Published in the United States

ISBN 978-1-7370168-0-9

follow MobytheFlea on Instagram

A Heartstone Paperback Original

Cover painting by Ron Richter

Amy Hill
amyhill999@yahoo.com

MOBY THE FLEA

AMY HILL

To produce a mighty book you must choose a mighty theme. No great and enduring volume can ever be written on the flea, though many there be who have tried it.

-Herman Melville

I

ASPIRATIONS

After going through a bad breakup and finding no one of interest on any dating site, Kevin thought he would get a dog. A dog would be just the thing to steady his nerves and shake off the blues. Whenever he found a permanent scowl on his face, whenever he caught himself yelling at his television screen, whenever he was becoming irritated with babies, it was time to make a change. Yes, his iPhone, his tablet and his MacBook Pro gave him much pleasure, and he heartily engaged with others on a variety of social media platforms, but in the center of his life was an ever-widening hole that needed to be filled. If companionship was the root of all happiness, he saw no reason this happiness should not come from a pet.

Though he had never owned one, he sensed that the endless struggle to find compatibility, so difficult with another human being, would not exist with a dog. Dogs were low maintenance, self-entertaining creatures who made few demands and did not impose their opinions on others. A dog would not care how much money he earned, a dog would not push him to reach higher goals, a dog would allow him to live his life as he wanted to.

He was tormented with an itch for the unfamiliar. The joyful cuddliness of a dog and all its attending marvels helped maintain his resolve. He envisioned happy times together, afternoons at the dog park, nights on his Posturepedic in front of

HBO. With a dog at my side, Kevin thought, I will never be alone. He and I will face this cruel world together.

II

THE ANIMAL SHELTER

It was a dark, dismal and bitingly cold Saturday in February. Kevin, dressed in layers of down, fleece and Thinsulate, tucked his wallet into his pocket and headed outside. Head down against blustery winds and clutching the neck of his jacket, he made his way north on Manhattan Street then turned onto Nanford Avenue.

Many candidates for dog ownership prefer a purebred, but his mind was made up. Only a mixed breed would do. There was something fine and boisterous about a mutt. His would be lively and brown, with maybe some terrier in his ancestry, some boxer to make him reliable, some beagle to make him sweet-tempered and some collie to keep him loyal.

After moving past buildings of various heights and conditions, he finally came to the address he was looking for, an odd looking structure, sadly leaning over, that might have been carted from the ruins of some war-torn country. It stood on a bleak corner where howling winds accompanied a chorus of forlorn barking. On a sign above the door, a painting of a tall, straight Doberman stood over the words "Animal Shelter." The swinging sign with its poverty-stricken creak to it told him this was the very place for a mutt.

He walked a short hallway then entered a room where behind a partition sat a young woman who appeared grateful to see him. He approached and told her of his wish to adopt a dog. She said there were more than enough to choose from if he had the time.

"What's your name?" she said.

"Call me Kevin."

The woman took his information, then led him down a long hallway lined with narrow cages. Black, brown and white faces turned to peer at them through their bars. Some barked sounding friendly, others with a pitch and duration he could not interpret. Too cheerful, he thought, watching a spaniel-like dog wag its tail. Too winsome, he told himself eyeing a sweet-eyed, fluffy-haired puppy.

But further down the aisle, in a large cage where four dogs resided, one immediately caught his interest. He held himself somewhat aloof, and his expression implied a reluctance to spoil the hilarity of his cage mates. He stood a full twelve inches high with floppy ears and a square nose. His deep brown fur made his white teeth dazzle by contrast, and his eyes were filled with reminiscences that seemed to puzzle him. Kevin approached the cage calling to him and at first received no response, but then the dog gave him a friendly bark.

"Miss," Kevin said, "what kind of dog is he—is he a mutt?"

"Yes," she answered. His father, she told him, a mixed breed as well, was thought to have good blood in his veins, though sadly vitiated by a fear of guns and thunder. His mother, mostly Golden Retriever, may have been responsible for his intelligence and good temper. He was one year old and completely housebroken.

Holding him, Kevin felt a mystical vibration. He was small and his tail wagged so hard, he named him Weewag and wrote the name in the pound registry. The woman sold him a red collar and leash and informed him of the services the pound provided, including obedience workshops, meditation for dogs, confidence-raising and doggie playgroups. And as young dogs are susceptible to many contagious and possibly deadly diseases, and as Weewag was due for his rabies and DHPP shots, she recommended Kevin have him immediately vaccinated. She knew of a particular veterinarian he might bring the dog to and assured him he was the best in Nanford. "In short," she said, "you couldn't do better." But Kevin was puzzled by the directions she gave him to his office. "Keep the McDonalds on your right, until you pass a white church on your left, until you arrive at a Shell station three blocks north, then ask the first person you meet where the place is. The doctor's name is Ahab."

III

DR AHAB

After wrapping himself and his dog in his shaggy jacket, Kevin emerged from the pound ready to combat a raging storm. At times blinded by furious gusts of rain, sleet and snow, he tried his best to follow the woman's directions. No one remained on the streets to ask for help, but he was able to catch sight of the few landmarks she had referred to and finally arrived at what was unmistakably the address he was looking for.

He felt a crick in his neck as he gazed at its ominous stature. He couldn't help sensing a vague misgiving. Long-seasoned and weather-stained, the facade was as dark as if exposed to the fumes of a thousand buses. He pushed through the building's heavy wooden doors and, shaking the sleet from his ice-glazed jacket, crossed the dusky entry into a hallway with such heavy beams above and such old planks beneath him, he imagined himself on some old sea vessel. He walked a long hallway and found a door that read "Veterinary Clinic." He entered a waiting room the silence of which was infrequently broken by the rustle of magazine pages and shrieks of the storm. The pet owners there seemed to sit purposely apart from each other, each with their own incommunicable concern. Two plaques on the wall next to the receptionist's desk read:

> Sacred to the memory of Whiskers who at the
> age of twelve was hit by a sixteen- wheeler in

6

Tuck Town. This plaque was hung by his dear and devoted owner, Jose, November 1, 20--.

Sacred to the memory of Lucky who at the age of seventeen keeled over in a Kmart parking lot. This plaque was hung by his loving owner, Meredith, January, 20—.

Standing under the cold blue fluorescents, as Kevin read about the sorry fates of the pets, he could barely imagine the desolation brooding in the hearts of their owners. Though Weewag could not read the dismal inscriptions, a wondrous curiosity seemed to fill his face. Yes, Weewag, Kevin thought, this fate may one day be ours.

But somehow his mood lifted. It's true, he thought, that a dog's life is shorter than a man's, but what of it? We have plenty of years before us.

Behind the front desk sat a long, thin, earnest looking woman, one who had spent forty years on Nanford's barren terrain. But her lack of physical excess wasn't the result of anxiety or any kind of ailment, it was only the condensation of her. She wasn't bad looking, almost the opposite. Her pure, dark skin was an excellent fit, and she brimmed with inner health. A gold hoop hung from each of her ears, and her braided hair coiled on top of her head. Her desk plate read "Quiznos."

When Kevin approached she looked up. "May I help you?"

"I just adopted this dog from the pound. He needs rabies and DHPP shots."

"Have you owned a dog before?"

"No, I haven't."

"Do you know anything about owning a dog?"

"Not much, but I'm sure I can learn. Growing up I had some fish. And a pet squirrel in my back yard—"

"A squirrel, and a few guppies in a bowl?" she said. "You think you can get by on your good looks alone? Have you thought about the responsibility of owning a dog, the cost, the risks of it?"

"I want to see what having a dog is like."

"Have you seen Dr. Ahab? If you want to know, I can tell you now, before you go in. Take a look at the doctor, young man, and you'll see. He's not a well man. He has only one eye."

"What do you mean? How did he lose the other one?"

"You know about pets and fleas?"

"Yes," Kevin said, "I have a friend who has a dog—"

"Don't aggravate me, please. I'm trying to tell you how hard it can be to own a dog. Do you think you're up to combing his fur for the nasty bug, to spraying him with flea spray?"

"I can, if I have to."

"Okay. Now you not only want to own a pet, but you also want to take care of him. Look at these people sitting here. What do you see?"

For a moment Kevin stood, puzzled by this request. But concentrating all her crows feet into a single scowl, she prodded him. Turning, he perceived that same air of worry and anxiety he had first sensed upon entering. He turned back to her.

"Anguish," he said, "and worry."

"So what do you think? Do you want to suffer just like these miserable people? Can't you go through life alone?"

He was staggered but determined, which he told the woman.

"Okay, then." She handed him a clipboard of forms to fill out. "Take a seat."

For most of the hour he and Weewag sat there, Kevin tried to amuse himself browsing the pages of *Pet Gazette* and *Modern Dog,* intermittently reassuring his dog with pats on the head. Slowly each owner and pet left the room until only the two of them remained, until suddenly a man in a white coat stood in the doorway.

"Kevin?" It was Dr. Ahab.

He did not appear to be ill or to be recovering from any illness. His high, broad form seemed made of steel and shaped in an unalterable mold. He might have just escaped a fire that had wasted his limbs without consuming them or depleting an ounce of their aged robustness. Kevin was so taken by his grimness, he was barely affected by the black patch covering his right eye. His left eye focused on him with an unblinking intensity.

Quiznos stopped typing and waited for the doctor to speak. She showed an uneasy if not painful consciousness of working for a troubled employer.

"You say your dog has fleas?" he said in a voice weary, yet hopeful.

Kevin turned, but found no one behind him. "Fleas? No. I came for vaccinations against rabies and DHPP."

"For you or the dog?"

Again, he looked at the doctor askance. This was his sense of humor. "The dog, of course."

"You know about fleas?"

"I suppose so."

"Well, you have to be careful about them. You know what to do if you see a flea?"

"Buy a flea collar?"

"No, you call me. Immediately. Many have single-handedly fought the flea and lost. They have overspent on inferior products and accomplished nothing. Only an experienced professional like myself can take care of the problem. All dogs are born with a thick layer of fur the flea likes to nest in. It's when they attack that you realize the silent perils of life. Now follow me."

Kevin, puzzled by such passionate advice, picked up Weewag and trailed after the doctor into the bowels of the clinic, to a room dominated by an oversized photo of the face of a Chihuahua hanging on the wall above the sink and a large, silver table that looked as if any smooth-pawed or sharp-nailed animal would slip and slide all over it. The room, intended for the examination of animals, lacked a single soft edge and resembled a showcase for stainless steel objects and laminate surfaces. But those objects shined with cleanliness, and the smell of disinfectants tickled Kevin's nose.

Dr. Ahab instructed him to place Weewag on the table and hold him there and, while the dog squirmed and squeaked, administered the shots requested. Then he reiterated that if Weewag should engage in the slightest episode of scratching, he should call him immediately.

"You have my number?" he said. It was already in Kevin's phone.

At the reception desk, after Kevin took care of the bill, Quiznos said, "The doctor gave your dog the vaccines you wanted?"

"He did."

"And he told you about fleas?"

"He did. But why all the concern about fleas? Is there a flea epidemic?"

"He didn't tell you?"

"Tell me what?"

She drew closer. "It's about the doctor's eye."

"He lost it to a dog who had fleas?"

"No. He lost it to a flea. A very nasty flea. His eye was devoured, chewed up, crunched by the smallest pest that ever glommed onto another being. He thought it jumped back onto the spaniel he was treating, but he never found it."

Kevin suddenly realized the doctor was beside him, he had no idea for how long. "So, Dr. Ahab," he said, looking up at him, "I'll see you in a year."

"A year? Maybe sooner. Are you employed, young man?"

"No, not at the moment. I was looking for a job, but now that I have a new pet, I may wait until—"

"Do you have experience with animals?"

"Yes, a little." He held back from telling him about his goldfish and squirrel.

"I could use some assistance. You look like an able-bodied young man."

"But I wouldn't want to abandon my new dog."

"Three days a week. You live close by, so you can go home for lunch. You should teach your dog independence."

Kevin's savings were diminishing. He could certainly use a job now, with another mouth to feed. "Are there health benefits?"

"No, no health benefits, not for part-time."

Kevin considered this for a few seconds but, as he rarely needed to see a doctor, told him three days a week would be fine.

"Good." The doctor turned to his receptionist. "Well, Quiznos," he said, "what should we pay this young man?"

Without taking her eyes off her computer screen, Quiznos replied. "You know best, Doctor."

"Fifteen an hour wouldn't be too little, would it?"

She looked up at him. "Fifteen? Frankly it's low, and considering the number of hours you're asking him to come in—"

"Fifteen an hour, Quiznos."

"Well, blast your eye, Dr. Ahab," Quiznos said. "You don't want to cheat this young man. He should have more than that."

"Fifteen an hour," the doctor repeated. "Where your treasure is, your heart will be too."

"I'll put him down for twenty," Quiznos said. "D'you hear that, Dr. Ahab? Twenty an hour."

Dr. Ahab turned solemnly towards her. "Quiznos, you have a generous heart, but if we reward the labors of this young man too abundantly we will ruffle the other workers. Fifteen, Quiznos."

Quiznos got up and began to clatter about her space. "Damn you, Dr. Ahab. If I always followed your advice, my guilty conscience would grow so large my head would explode."

"Quiznos," Dr. Ahab said, "Your conscience is already so large I'm surprised it doesn't tip you over. And he'll get free treatments for his dog for as long as he works for me." He turned and spoke to Kevin. "I'll see you at nine tomorrow morning."

Kevin stepped aside to let the doctor pass, no doubt eager to escape the wrath of his receptionist.

As soon as he was gone, Quiznos said, "Kevin's your name, did you say?"

She handed him another clipboard, this time with a stack of papers to sign, which he did, not bothering to read them. Doubtless he had come into a good thing. This job might not make him rich, but he had never cared about riches.

The storm had subsided and the sun was peeking out from behind the clouds. With his new pet tucked back inside his jacket, Kevin headed home, skirting drips and puddles. Thoughts of the doctor filled his mind. He felt a strange mixture of pity and awe for him, as he knew so little about him. But he was soon distracted by a shopping trip to Howlistic, the local pet store, where he bought a ball and the dog food the clerk recommended, and Dr. Ahab was for the moment forgotten.

IV

NANFORD

He lived in Nanford, full of mini-malls, chain stores and parking lots, a town so small, it could only be found on MapQuest after tapping many times on the plus sign. The town was so built up and paved in every way, it had become an utter rock. It was covered in more asphalt and concrete than could be used in twenty years, and grew so little foliage and so few trees that one blade of grass made a garden and three made a park. Not a single rake could be found in Nanford, not one garden supply store.

Founded on a deposit of limestone and clay, it was home to many proud creators of cement dishware, planters and paperweights. The townspeople spoke of the concreteness of things and often cemented relationships. They took classes in crafting concrete at Nanford's high school, also made of the same hardy material. In the town square, surrounded by the concrete bank, liquor store and town hall, stood a concrete sculpture of Johann Strauss who had once passed through Nanford on tour with his orchestra.

No wonder so many residents chose to live with a pet. Pets provided a taste of the natural world many craved. Most owned a dog or a cat, while birds, rabbits and even snakes were not unpopular. In Nanford less insects were stepped on than in any neighboring greener towns.

His apartment was on Manhattan Street, on the third floor of a five-story concrete building. Once inside, under the kitchen sink, Weewag sniffed the corroding pipes, in the living room he clawed at the Indian throw rug, and in the bathroom he spent some time inspecting the base of the toilet. Then Kevin emptied half of a can of beef-flavored food into a metal bowl that his dog downed quickly and with an audible relish, as if trying to fill a vacancy created by the lack of some previous meal. Kevin watched Weewag as he ate and found his head phrenologically excellent, with long retreating slopes from above the brows, like two promontories. He was a simple animal with a lofty bearing, Kevin thought. What a pity his peaceful and happy existence might be destroyed by a tiny insect, one he was so ignorant of.

He sat before his laptop. The flea, he found, is a wingless ectoparasite, a tiny brown insect with a siphon-like mouthpart used to penetrate the skin of a host animal and drink its blood. Different kinds of fleas live off the blood of different animals, such as raccoons, possums, deer, cattle, coyotes, foxes, bobcats, skunks, ferrets, panthers, mice, squirrels, armadillos, poultry, birds, rats, dogs, cats, pigs, bats, horses, goats, and sheep. Google images showed the little bug as odd and ugly-looking.

At eleven p.m. as soon as Kevin got into bed, Weewag sprang onto the blanket beside him. Kevin never slept better in his life. He woke the next morning in his cold room to find the dog still beside him, his fur-covered body supplying much-needed warmth. Suddenly Weewag roused, gave himself a good stretching, sneezed twice and jumped to the floor. As he circled, then scratched on the bedroom door, Kevin understood he needed to relieve himself. Dogs have an innate sense of delicacy, he thought. They're wonderfully polite.

After a quick walk then a simple breakfast, he told his dog good-bye, promising to be back in three hours. He made sure the curtains were open so he could look out the front windows and, though the view offered few trees and little wildlife, he could watch the cars and people go by. As Kevin backed out of his apartment, his dog sat with his tail in half a wag and a questioning look in his eyes. It was possible that raised in a pound, he had never spent a moment alone. Kevin might be imposing his own desires onto his pet, but it pained him to leave him without a good book to read.

V

INITIATION

Just before the doors of Dr. Ahab's office building closed behind him, someone practically leapt inside. Kevin turned to see a young man squeezing past him, then stopping to face him, blocking his way.

"Going to see Ahab?" He had high cheek bones and squinty, black eyes with a glittering expression. His pointy ears seemed to cut like knives through his dark locks of hair. He was not going to let Kevin pass until he received an answer.

"Yes, Dr. Ahab. It's my first day of work there."

He was shabbily dressed in a faded jean jacket and patched jeans. "Work? Sign any papers? Make sure you don't sign away your soul. Or perhaps you haven't got one, perhaps." He spoke with a jittery cadence. "No matter though, I know a lot of people who don't. Good luck to them, and they're probably better off without one. A soul's a sort of a fifth wheel to a car, it is."

"I have no idea what you're talking about." Kevin tried passing him, but the young man leapt to the right, blocking him once more.

"He's got enough deficiencies to make up for all the ones in other people, he does," the man said, emphasizing the word 'he.'

"He? You mean Dr. Ahab?" Thinking he must have just broken loose from a psych ward, Kevin again tried to push past him. This time the man moved to the left, blocking him again.

"I'm Rodney. I'll be working with you, yes, Rodney." He extended his hand to shake.

Kevin questioned Dr. Ahab's discretion in hiring his workers. He found it hard to believe such a man was in the doctor's employ. "I'm Kevin," he said, shaking his hand. "I'll be working Mondays, Wednesdays and Fridays."

"So you've met Old Thunder?"

"Who's Old Thunder?"

"Dr. Ahab. Some of us in the clinic call him that. You've met him I suppose?
And what do you know about him? Anything?"

"I hear he's sick but it seems he's getting better."

"Getting better!" Rodney's laugh was derisive. "When Dr. Ahab is better, my dead dog will be better, she will."

"I'm sorry about your dog, but I hear he's a good vet. He seems to have a successful business."

"Yes, he seems to, he does. But if you're going to work for him, you have to jump when he gives an order. Get cracking, hop to it—that's the word with Dr. Ahab. But nothing about him losing his eye to the flea, nothing? The one that jumped off the Cocker Spaniel? I mean you know he has only one eye and that a flea took the other, you know."

"Yes, I know all about the loss of his eye."

"All about it? Are you sure?"

"Pretty sure."

Rodney gave him a suspicious look. "You say you signed? Name on the paper, you say? Well, what's signed is signed, and what will be, will be. Anyhow, it's all arranged. Good Morning. Best of luck to you. Sorry to delay you, sorry."

He spun on his heel, but intrigued by his words, Kevin stopped him. "Hey, look, if you have anything to tell me, tell me now."

"It's sad," he said, "but you're just the man for him, you are. And God bless us, so am I. Good morning."

Before he turned again, Kevin said, "If there's something I should know, I think you should tell me."

"Morning to you. Morning."

"Morning it is." Kevin followed the peculiar man to Dr. Ahab's door. Inside, Quiznos nodded to Rodney when he passed her desk, he responded with the same "Morning" then headed down the hallway that led to the examination room.

She looked up when Kevin drew near, then pressed on a lever of a boxlike object sitting on her desk. "Kevin is here," she called into it.

This produced a long, fuzzy grunt. Years of working here had apparently familiarized her with its meaning.

"Have a seat," she said. "The doctor will be right with you."

But his nerves, rattled by the encounter with the unfathomable Rodney, might be soothed by a sane conversation. He addressed the busy woman. "Quiznos? What's working with Dr. Ahab like?"

She stopped typing and removed her glasses showing sentimental eyes. She took a breath and spoke in low tones. "I've worked for him twenty-two years," she said. "I don't know exactly what's wrong with him, but he keeps to himself. He doesn't look sick, but he is...sort of. Or maybe he isn't sick, but he isn't well, either. He's an odd person, but a good one. I think you'll like him. He doesn't talk much, but when he does, you listen. He's not cheerful, and ever since that damned flea attacked him, he went a little crazy, but it must have been the pains in his eye. He became kind of moody and strange, but that won't last. And I promise you, it's better to work for a moody, good doctor than a cheerful, bad one. He was once married and had a son. His wife is dead now, but she was a sweet woman and extremely devoted to him. And when Rodney's dog died, he arranged the funeral. There's no harm in Dr. Ahab. He has his humanity! So try to—"

The buzz of the intercom interrupted her. "Yes?" After listening to three unintelligible syllables, she said to Kevin, "He'll see you in his office. Down the hall, first room on your right."

Kevin followed her directions and entered a small office of the sparest wooden furnishings, where an iMac and its keyboard sat on a wide desk surrounded by a clutter of medical books, papers and a half-filled pack of Marlboro 100's. Dr. Ahab stood behind it, looking out his open window, inhaling on a cigarette. Hearing Kevin he turned, as a thick vapor streamed from his mouth.

"What the hell," he said, half to himself, withdrawing the cigarette from his lips. "Smoking no longer does it for me. Why smoke if it's lost its appeal? It's become a habit, not a pleasure. I've been smoking with nervous whiffs like a dying insect. What business do I have doing it? This pastime is meant for a younger man, not an old grey man like me."

He tossed the cigarette, then the entire pack out the window and, for a few seconds, gazed out at the objects as they disappeared below. Then he sat at his desk.

"Have a seat," he told Kevin, and spoke as he joined him, in a mild voice of unassuming authority. "Looking for fleas is a disreputable pursuit. It's not a cerebral profession. Some call it ridiculous. It's basically murder—"

This man certainly has it out for fleas, Kevin said to himself. Yes, he must resent the loss of his eye, but it seems more than prominent in his mind. I'm sure there are more important aspects to animal medicine I should know.

A ringing interrupted his thoughts, sounding like a worn bell, whose source he soon managed to identify, a chipped, black push-button phone sitting near the doctor's elbow. Dr. Ahab picked up a receiver whose corroded mouthpiece appeared to suffer from years of exposure to breathing.

"Hello!" he said, as though shouting through a megaphone. "Goney!" He listened attentively for a few seconds. "Crozette? No, I haven't seen any dog named Crozette. . .Yes? . . .And what did you find? Any fleas? . . .No?" With his face in a grimace, he listened a few seconds before hanging up. "Damn cell phones." He turned to Kevin. "These newfangled contraptions cause a lot of aggravation. And what does it lead to?"

"Will you call him back?"

"I have no reason to."

In anticipation of a challenging day, Kevin had drunk an extra cup of coffee that morning and asked to use the men's room. He passed Quiznos on the way and updated her on their progress—or lack of it.

"He got a call from someone named Goney," he told her, "but it was cut short and he's not calling him back."

"Goney is a fellow vet," she said. "They've been friends since med school. They never spoke that often but, when they used to, they could talk for hours. They had a lot in common and a lot to complain about, like the usual pet ailments and any news in the vet world. But since his accident, Dr. Ahab has changed. Ordi-

21

narily he would have called Dr. Goney back. But now he doesn't want to socialize with anyone, even for five minutes."

When Kevin returned to the office, he found it empty and soon discovered Dr. Ahab in the examination room with Rodney who was brushing the coat of a Golden Retriever standing patiently on the examination table.

Dr. Ahab spoke to Kevin. "You know how to search for fleas?"

His preoccupation with the insect was beginning to appear an obsession, Kevin thought. "I don't," he said.

"Rodney," Dr. Ahab said, "this is Kevin. I need to teach him about inspecting for fleas."

Rodney squinted at Kevin. "Yes, we've met, we have," he said.

Dr. Ahab directed Kevin to hold the dog around her neck. "First do a visual examination," he said, running a bony finger along the dog's back, revealing the roots of the thick fur. "A flea is small, but not microscopic, so you can spot one with your naked eye. He wears his skeleton on the outside, like a coat of armor, so don't waste your time trying to crush one between your fingers. Nor can one be destroyed by the teeth of any animal."

He picked up an odd-looking comb with a green handle. "This is the flea comb, a comb with closely set teeth. A larger separation between the teeth would allow the flea to slip through it. Fleas have hairs on their back that act like velcro, so they can stick to a dog's fur. This comb will help you pull them out. Run the comb over the dog's back from head to tail," he said as he did so. "Comb the legs from the top to the paw. Press hard to get close to the skin. Now help me turn the dog over."

The dog appeared to be getting on in years and showed no

resistance when they placed her on her back and held her still.

"Fleas like to live in the warmest and most protected areas of an animal," the doctor went on, "like the hind end, the armpits and groin. Look for red or bumpy skin, also for hair loss and scabbing. Have a bowl of soapy water nearby where you can drop the fleas so if you catch one on your comb. The soap breaks down the water resistance of the exoskeleton causing the flea to sink and drown." He tore off a paper towel and went to the sink to moisten it. Kevin held the dog securely while the doctor ran the comb over her stomach and the insides of her legs. "After using the comb, if you didn't find any fleas, transfer any debris to a moist towel," he said. "If the dirt dissolves into a red color, it's flea dirt, so you'll have to search again." After he ran the comb over the towel it remained perfectly white, which seemed to cause a look of disappointment in the doctor's one eye. "You can catch the fleas with the comb, or spray them with one of the sprays in the cabinet, depending on the magnitude of the infestation."

"I understand."

"Now Rodney will tell you the rest." Dr. Ahab was soon heading out of the room.

Within the confines of the medical clinic and under Dr. Ahab's supervision, Rodney showed a calmer demeanor than he had in the hallway. Kevin soon learned he had been working in Dr. Ahab's clinic for fourteen years after earning a degree as a veterinary assistant. His dog, a Chihuahua named Natasha, the subject of the photo hanging in the room, had recently died of kidney disease at the age of nineteen.

Kevin studied the photo, the large scale of the face causing the small and cute dog to look grotesque and menacing. "Will you ever get another dog?"

"Replace her?" Rodney said.

"Well I wouldn't put it—"

"No, impossible."

Rodney calmly continued listing the duties Kevin would be required to perform such as taking stock of supplies and keeping the cotton ball, tongue depressor and Q-tips jars full.

"Natasha was irreplaceable, she was," he finally said. "There was no dog like her, none."

He lead Kevin to the employee room then the rooms where medications were stored, where X-rays were taken, where the doctor performed minor procedures, where blood samples were drawn and where the laundry was done. Later Kevin would receive instruction on how to bathe the animals, trim nails, clip hair, brush teeth and attend to other grooming needs.

"Are you familiar with brushing a dog?" Rodney held up a two-sided hairbrush. "Of course you're familiar. The steel side removes loose hair and tangles, yes, and the soft side spreads natural oils over the dog's coat." To Kevin's relief, it had been at least a half hour since fleas had been mentioned. But after showing him how much pressure to use while brushing, Rodney said, "You know about the jump of the flea?"

"The jump? No, I don't."

"Be careful about the jump," Rodney said. "Be careful. A flea can jump up to ten inches in the air and thirteen inches horizontally, equal to a human jumping over the Capitol Building, it can."

"Wow. I had no idea."

"A flea can jump 30,000 times without stopping. Entomologists are fascinated by this jump. They've spent years trying to figure it out, they have. Have you seen the videos?"

"What videos?"

"The videos of fleas jumping. You can watch them for hours, you can. Ten, nine, eight, seven, six, five, four, three, two, one, blast off!" His hand gestured upwards. "They blast into space like tiny rocket ships."

Kevin could no longer stop himself from asking the question burning in his mind. "Why so much talk about fleas? I understand about the doctor's accident, but aren't there other things I should be concerned about?"

Rodney's mouth opened and closed. It was odd to see someone so full of words grasping for them. "I thought you knew."

"Knew what?"

"No on told you?"

"Told me what?"

He took a breath. "The flea that took the doctor's eye was white, it was."

"I thought all fleas were brown."

"Not this one, no. I was there when it happened. I saw the flea myself. It was white, all right, as white as a bolt of lightning."

"And the doctor wants to find this particular flea?"

"Yes, with every bone in his body, he wants to. He even has a name for the insect, Moby."

"After Moby Dick, the whale?"

Rodney looked puzzled. "The whale? No, the singer, Moby. You know Moby, you must. Dr. Ahab hates when Quiznos puts in her earbuds and listens to him, he does. She can't hear the doctor or anyone else if they need her. He saw the name Moby on one of her CDs, he did, so now the word 'Moby' signifies anything the doctor hates. We once had Moby the dog and Moby the UPS guy who mixed up all the packages, yes, the UPS guy."

"And he wants to kill this white flea?"

"Kill it dead. Deader than anything that ever died before. Murder it, spray it, squash it, take the last living breath out of it, that's what Dr. Ahab wants."

"But how long does a flea live?"

"Long enough. A flea's life can be long, it can. Some fleas die in a few months, but if it can find the right food, like blood and waste and flea feces, a flea can live for up to a year, even two. And if it can't find a meal, it can eat the food it stored inside itself, it can. There's a good chance Moby is still alive. And if he isn't, the search will go on anyway. It's better to search for a dead flea than not search at all, much better. So if you're searching a dog and you see a white flea you call us over, me and the doctor, immediately."

Busy replenishing supplies then taking notes on which were running low, Kevin was unable to immediately contemplate Rodney's words, though in the back of his mind lay something strange and ominous. Finally as he made his way home for lunch, he had time to ponder this odd revelation. He had been thrown into an extraordinary if not bizarre situation he might want to escape from before being sucked too deeply into it. Now Rodney's words in the hallway made more sense. Kevin stopped in his tracks. Was this the reason Dr. Ahab had hired him?

But what did it matter as long as he performed whatever duties were assigned to him in exchange for the agreed-upon compensation? Yes, continuing to work for Dr. Ahab implied his involvement in the silly search, but he could easily distance himself from it. Kevin had always been resistant to seduction. He rarely overate, drank alcohol and did not enjoy mood-altering drugs. He didn't gamble or subscribe to any organized religion. He might catch a cold or a flu, but never Moby fever.

He would continue to perform whatever asked of him until six p.m., including the searching of dogs for a specific insect the doctor took issue with. He had no problem with that insect. It was an insect like any other.

His eagerness to be reunited with his new housemate soon overtook his concerns. As soon as he opened his apartment door, his dog began barking, leaping at him and circling him with a ferociously wagging tail. But his living room floor was strewn with bits and shreds of the foam from inside his couch pillows, in the bedroom he discovered his favorite jeans had been chewed at the waist and the bathroom floor was covered with shreds of toilet paper.

"Weewag! Bad dog!" Kevin said as his dog sat amidst the living room mess, as if proud of his efforts at interior decoration. But even before cleaning up and assessing the problem, Kevin would subject his pet to the procedure he had been contemplating all day. He found a comb with teeth probably too widely spaced, but one that would do.

"Stay still, Weewag," he said as he ran the comb through the thick fur on the dog's back and legs. Weewag stood still enough, seeming to enjoy the sensation. After a thorough search of his entire coat, Kevin was relieved to find not a single flea on him.

After a quick lunch and clean-up, before returning to the clinic, he shut his bedroom and bathroom doors tightly. "Be back soon," he told Weewag, hoping he might grow to trust that he would. But four hours later, when he returned and, after surviving another enthusiastic welcome, he saw his dog had chewed the side of his armchair, decorating the floor with its cottony filling. "Weewag!" Kevin wondered if he had chosen the wrong dog.

On Kevin's second day of work, he met Kit, also recently hired, small and fragile with a tattoo of Gandalf on his forearm and excellent computer skills. But under the rule of Dr. Ahab and the periodic requests of Rodney to interact with this or that oversized, sharp-toothed, sharp-nailed dog, his time in the clinic had become one continual lip-quiver. Had the duties of the job been better explained, Kit would never have accepted it.

That afternoon, a large mixed breed resembling a spotless Dalmatian with a mysterious skin rash was brought in, and Rodney insisted Kit search him for fleas. "A flea search. Prepare a bowl of soapy water and comb him down. Yes, comb him."

Kit, like Kevin, had been well and thoroughly instructed by the doctor on how to proceed with a search, but at the thought of his own personal one, his eyes grew round with terror. Among established phobias of insects are fears of bees, ants, moths and butterflies. There is no phobia linked specifically to fleas, but if there were one, Kit was stricken with it. While Rodney watched and Kevin held the dog by the neck, the entomophobic Kit prepared the bowl of soapy water and picked up the flea comb with apprehension. His nerves calmed as he began to run the comb down the dog's long back, creating wakes in the sea of short white fur. But when he reached the hind end, hidden deep in the hairs, tiny, ugly crawlers appeared to be eating the poor dog alive. He flung the comb high in the air and backed away, panting.

"I can't do it," he cried, his skin white, his hands trembling. "I can't! Oh, those ugly fleas!"

"Ugly fleas?" Rodney said. "Wait till you see the maggots!"

He picked up the comb and handed it to Kevin. As Kevin proceeded with the search, he found the sight of the fleas unpleasant, but felt satisfaction in relieving the anguish of the dog.

When Dr. Ahab learned of Kit's phobia, he eyed him with disappointment. But even Rodney was forced to admit Kit's computer skills far surpassed even his own. "From now on," Dr. Ahab told Kit, "you'll deal with the computer and leave the fleas to the rest of us."

"The files, not the fleas," Rodney said.

VI

THE PEP TALK

After one week in Dr. Ahab's clinic, Kevin had conducted twenty-three flea searches, most without the knowledge of the pets' owners. "We don't ask," Dr. Ahab said, "at the risk of a denial of permission." Kevin questioned the ethicality of this, but he would obey his employer, certainly a better judge of the strictness and enforcement of the rules of the American Veterinary Medical Association than he was. After all, as far as he could tell, a flea search could only benefit and in no way harm a dog. So far, he had found an average of five fleas per dog, that most dogs were completely clean and few had small infestations. He had seen no sign of a white flea or a flea of any other color but a deep reddish brown.

The following Monday near the end of the workday, Dr. Ahab called to his crew to assemble in the examination room. Quiznos' inclusion implied the meeting's importance. As he paced before them, with the black patch over his right eye, he resembled a pirate plotting his next attack. He grew still and turned to them, his left eye traveling from face to face.

"What do you do when you see a white flea?"

"Call you over!" the group answered, then looked curiously at each other, as if amazed at their excitement over such a ridiculous question.

"Good!" Dr. Ahab was pleased with the hearty animation his unexpected question had thrown them into. "And what do you do next?"

"Grab the insecticide!"

"Good again!"

"And what do you do if you find Moby and kill him?"

"Wrap him in a paper towel!"

At every response the old man's expression grew even more glad. "Whoever spots the White Flea will be well paid. A raise plus benefits, including the Blue Cross Blue Shield Advantage Plan."

"Awesome! Okay!" Kit and Rodney cried.

"He's a white flea," Dr. Ahab resumed. "Skin your eyes for him, look sharp. If you catch even a glimpse of him, call me over."

"Yes!" they shouted to the excited old man. "A sharp eye for the White Flea, a good spray at Moby the Flea!"

"Dr. Ahab," Kit said. "You call him Moby?"

"Yes, Moby," the doctor said. "You know him then, Kit?"

"He's the one that can jump as high as the Empire State Building," Kit said.

"And is covered with insecticide," Rodney added.

"Yes, that's Moby. He's the damned white flea that got me, that leapt out of the spaniel's fur and bit my eyelid, making me half-blind forever. It'll be a trial and an undertaking, but I'll find him. I'm searching every dog that comes into this clinic. I'm checking the dog park and all the pet stores in the area. And I'm asking you to help me, to chase that cursed flea over all the dogs in this town. Rodney, go to the refrigerator. You'll find some beers in there."

Dr. Ahab had been aware of Quiznos watching with an uneasy expression. "Why the long face, Quiznos?" he called to her.

31

After a few seconds' thought, she came closer. "Dr. Ahab! Is this why I work for you? For vengeance? Even if you kill that damn flea, how much would you earn? Not much, even in a flea market!"

"Flea market! Ha! But if vengeance had value, it would earn me a good premium."

Rodney, returning from the kitchen with an armful of bottles of Rolling Rock, handed one to Kevin. "When he beats his chest," Rodney whispered, "it sounds hollow, it does."

They passed the bottles around while the doctor spoke. "The White Flea is like a wall to me, a wall I must break through. Sometimes I think there's nothing beyond it, but it's enough that he puts me to the task. I see outrageous strength in him, inscrutable malice. This isn't just about an eye. I have another eye. It's the inscrutability I hate. The White Flea is the agent of that hate, and I'll wreak it back at him."

"That bug didn't know what he was doing," Quiznos said. "He was acting on instinct. It doesn't seem fair."

"Don't talk to me about fairness," the doctor said. "I would strike the sun if it insulted me." He turned to the others. "Rodney, Kevin, Kit, are you with me? Quiznos, remove that anger from your face. It's a fleeting emotion you'll soon regret. You're like a weak tree in the middle of a hurricane. I need your help. Is it so hard to give?" He paused a moment, waiting for her response. "You say nothing," he said. "I think I know what that means." He lowered his voice and spoke to the rest of them as if Quiznos couldn't hear him. "Something I said got through to her. Quiznos has stopped opposing me. She's with us now."

"Damn you, Dr. Ahab!" Quiznos said. But her eyes lit with stubbornness. "Be careful," she said. "Those who obsess over winning the award forget the cost of getting it. Don't give yourself up to blind ambition."

But in his joy at her tacit acquiescence, Dr. Ahab did not sense the foreboding in her words, nor the low laugh from the rest of them, nor the warning vibrations of the winds against the windows. Turning to the rest, he ordered them to hold up their bottles. "Drink up!" he cried. "Short draughts—long swallows. It goes down well, spirals inside you. Well done, almost finished. It's like life. You gulp it and it's gone." He ran his eye from Quiznos to Rodney to Kit to Kevin as if trying to infuse them with the same charge he felt.

"Maybe you know how I feel. Maybe you share my feelings. Do you hate the struggle? It might kill you. You can decide for yourself to join me. I'm not ordering you. Do as you like. A toast!"

The five of them clicked bottles.

"Death to the White Flea!"

"Death to the White Flea!"

"We'll hunt Moby the Flea to his death!"

They shouted maledictions against the White Flea, then drank with one simultaneous swallow. They were like children running after a dog, the head child destined to trip over a crack in the sidewalk. When the doctor offered more beer, Quiznos looked pale and refused it. He waved to them, then headed down the hall to his office.

The talk had gone better than Dr. Ahab had expected. Not only had it spurred his crew on, but it increased his own resolve. He did find Quiznos stubborn, but the rest were like cogs that fit well in his wheel with the promise to circle at his will. He knew they considered him a madman, especially Quiznos, and he told himself, yes, perhaps they were right, but he was well aware of his madness. Like a boxer in the ring, he had been knocked down, but now he stood upright again. He had lost an eye, but now he would blind his blinder. The White Flea was out there somewhere in the universe, and he would summon him from among the tufts of fur he came across daily until the insect showed himself, perhaps at his own will. The doctor's path ahead lay newly paved, smooth as ice, and he would rush over it without a stumble.

After every work-day, Kevin tried to look forward to returning to Weewag, to spending welcome time away from Dr. Ahab's clinic, a place of torment and despair. But what warmth and affection he drew from his dog was marred by the continuation of his rampage of indiscriminate chewing. Back at Howlistic Kevin bought a spray the clerk guaranteed would render any surface repugnant to a dog, but though Kevin diligently used it, in a week's time, Weewag feasted on more of his armchair, two more pillows and was working on shredding the side of his couch. Whatever plastic coverings, sheets or blankets he used to safeguard his furniture also fell victim to the dog's teeth. Kevin returned to Howlistic where he bought a chew toy that once again the clerk promised would resolve the situation.

VII

BACKGROUND

The crew had shouted in unison, and the louder they shouted, the more they believed in their promise. The doctor's objective, however quenchless it appeared, was theirs. But there was fear in that shout. Kevin, eager to know more, with greedy ears, and by means of questioning and eavesdropping on his fellow employees, finally learned the details of the dreadful event that took place between Dr. Ahab and the monstrous flea.

It happened a full three weeks before Kevin was hired, when Dr. Ahab was tending to Trigger, a young Cocker Spaniel with a shiny nose and an abundant coat of black hair. Rodney held the dog still while the doctor prepared a syringe for a booster shot. At this time, even a horde of fleas residing on this dog would have been of little concern.

On the back of the dog near the rim of her collar, sat a flea of a very unexpected color. This flea had been feeding off the Cocker Spaniel for a few days now and had sucked about as much of her blood as he could tolerate. The blood had a strange aftertaste that grew to repulse him, that compelled him to find a new host. As the doctor's face drew near, the insect's antennae detected vibrations, his dim eyes saw a shadowy form and he sensed the carbon dioxide the old man exhaled. His appetite restored, he made his jump, adhered himself to the doctor's right eyelid, inserted his mouth parts and sucked. No vampire could have struck with more malice. In one long drink, he drew from the eye all the vitreous humor he could stomach. He found it delicious. Satisfied, he removed his mouth-parts, and detecting ominous shadows coming back at him, leapt back into the protection of the dog's coat.

Both the doctor and Rodney had seen the whiteness. It was the color of milk, Rodney said. The doctor who then had two good eyes, agreed. Later he said the flea was like a blinding light, so close in proximity there was no mistaking it. Rodney dialed 911 and an ambulance was on its way.

Much to Rodney's disappointment, Daniel Appletree, Trigger's owner, expressed little regret that the flea responsible for the doctor's calamity had leapt off his particular dog. "Did I do something wrong?" he said to Rodney after Dr. Ahab was wheeled out of the clinic and Rodney was left to tend his patients. "I can't help it if some crazy flea attaches itself to my dog, can I? Will the doctor sue me?"

Rodney assured Daniel he held no responsibility for the attack, that it was an occupational hazard, and that veterinarians often suffered injuries inflicted on them by their patients.

News of the terrible event spread to the rest of the veterinary community via texts, emails and phone calls. Long threads on Facebook discussed the horror of it.

"It could happen to any one of us," a fellow vet wrote. Many checked their insurance policies.

As the weeks went by, reports of fleas of uncommon whiteness and malignancy on this or that dog surfaced, but with no evidence to claim they were Moby. When those in the know caught sight of such a flea, they boldly and fearlessly sprayed it, but it inevitably escaped unharmed. Calamities such as sprained fingers, carpel tunnel syndrome or countless, tiny, itchy bites piled terrors on the White Flea, and fear shook the fortitude of even the bravest vets and dog owners.

Outrageous rumors persisted. Some said this event proved that fleas not only thirsted for animal blood, but for human blood too. Others called Moby the Flea ubiquitous, that he had been encountered on two different dogs at the same time. Still others referred to him as the "Teflon Flea" and declared him immortal. And to further invest him with terror, he was deemed an insect of some intelligence.

At the time of the attack, Dr. Ahab was only angered and not yet mad. But during his recovery, when he and his anguish lay together in one bed, his monomania seized him. His torn body and gashed spirit bled into one another. His madness came at odd intervals, and his delirium intensified. His neighbors, hearing his wails, wondered if they should have him committed. But in time the delirium cooled, and he emerged from it as from the dark into the light.

Back in the clinic he put on a good face (however pale), ran his practice in the same calm manner as before, and his employees thanked God the madness was gone. But beneath the surface, to no one's awareness, it raved on. Madness is a cunning phenomenon. Just when it appears to be gone, it has only changed color or form. Dr. Ahab's lunacy did not subside. It deepened, and not one iota of his intellect perished. His lunacy turned its gun against itself, and he was stronger than ever.

This strength enabled him to persuade every one of his employees to join him. For the two weeks Dr. Ahab took to recover, Rodney took his place, taking care of simple ailments like ear mites and stomach upsets, while pets with more advanced complaints were referred to Dr. Goney. Not until Dr. Ahab's return did Rodney realize the extent of his employer's transformation. He was appalled by his pallor, by the glumness of his once-friendly expression. But it was the eyepatch that most altered him, one made of a dull black fabric that appeared like a dark tunnel leading to an unnamable place.

"Did you find the White Flea?" the doctor greeted him, genially enough. "Did you see where it landed?" This confirmed Rodney's most dreaded fear, that the mind of Dr. Ahab had been taken hostage by insanity.

"I saw it jump back on the dog, I did," he said.

"And did you inspect the dog?"

"No, I didn't." Only his employer's condition had concerned him.

Dr. Ahab was assured his monocular vision would not prevent him from continuing his practice. He received therapy for his sight but not for his emotions. Even while learning how to pick up a coffee cup and judge the distance of a moving car, unwanted notions were invading his mind.

But a small shred of logic seeped in as well. As fleas were usually faithful to their host, the White Flea might still reside in the Cocker Spaniel's fur. It was only a matter of inspection, then extermination. Rodney had warned him about Daniel's reaction, but Dr. Ahab had no need for sympathy. He asked Quiznos to phone Daniel and request he bring Trigger to the clinic as soon as possible. "His dog hosted the flea that bit me. Tell him we have to make sure she's not hosting more. Assure him we don't hold him responsible."

The next day, while Daniel sat in the waiting room, Rodney searched Trigger thoroughly and discovered eleven fleas on her, none of them white.

"He's jumped to another dog," Dr. Ahab told Rodney before speaking with Daniel.

"Contact tracing," Rodney told him. "We need to do contact tracing, we do." The only way to find Moby, he said, was to discover which dogs Trigger had come into contact with since the attack. Dr. Ahab's lack of familiarity with the term did not stop him from assessing its meaning and relevance to his cause. Until now, his mania had prevented him from seeing this clear and pragmatic path to his goal.

"We'll search every dog that ever stepped into this town," he told Rodney, "until we find him."

Rodney's sympathy for his employer was deep and immutable. For fourteen years he worked side by side with the doctor, his advisor, his teacher, his spiritual brother. Dr. Ahab hired Rodney even before he finished earning his degree. He supported him through his grief for his dog and arranged her burial. No matter what the nature of his quest, no matter how outlandish, wild or preposterous, Rodney would join him with no question, no sense of obligation and no need for reward.

He called Daniel to the examination room, told him they had removed more fleas from Trigger's coat and were concerned about their spread in the community. "Fleas jump from dog to dog," he told Daniel, "Can you possibly tell us which dogs Trigger might have come into contact with, can you? Do you walk Trigger at particular times of the day?"

"No, I don't," Daniel said. "I sell real estate and I have no routine. I live with my wife and my daughter and we all take

Trigger out three times a day and walked him up and down Heg-nog Street."

This was cause for optimism. This small amount of territory would limit the number of dogs Trigger might run into. But then Daniel added that his daughter and Trigger had visited the dog park on one of the following weekends after his original visit to the clinic (he could not remember which), and Dr. Ahab's hopes diminished. Contacting and searching every dog they had passed on the way, not to mention every dog that frequented the park—with its random and unpredictable population—would be impossible. Contact tracing was therefore forced to be abandoned.

Kevin had been willing to accept the search for Moby as part of his job, but slow to realize its far reaching implications. At first the man in command seemed peculiar, perhaps eccentric, but he decided the psychological state of his employer was not his business. But as the weeks passed and the number of possible hosts that paraded in and out of the clinic steadily increased, Kevin became more and more sure of his own diagnosis. The doctor's condition could not be considered a slight deviation from normal behavior. It was far more extreme, to a dizzying degree, and it took some time to admit even to himself its true identity, monomania.

No matter, he told himself, reassuring himself of his capabilities for independent thinking, his tried and true resistance to persuasion. But as time went on, he soon found that at the end of each workday, he could not leave the doctor's obsession in the clinic coat closet and pick it up his next working morning. Even away from his workplace, his brain buzzed with thoughts of the quest. Though he tried to suppress it, "Have you seen the White Flea?" beat like a drum in his head. A special sickness was invading him, one he lacked the immunities to fight against.

During his next workday, about to conduct a flea search among the long and tangly hairs of an Afghan Hound, he suddenly felt frozen, almost paralyzed. Though he worked by bright fluorescent lights, darkness surrounded him, and in that gloom lurked a madness he was succumbing to. Though his eyes were open, he felt only half-conscious. Only despair lay ahead. However efficient the clinic, however many pets were healed or vaccinated there, a madman ruled it with no restraints, under no surveillance.

Kevin convulsively grasped the flea comb but perceived its teeth twisted and gnarled. What's wrong with me? he thought. A minute ago I could have sworn this dog was facing me, but now I see the back of him, and just in time to prevent him from jumping off the table. But I mustn't think about this now. Tomorrow the skies will brighten, the day will bring better thoughts and home will give me relief.

VIII

SEARCHING FOR FLEAS

It seemed a hopeless task to seek out one solitary creature from among Nanford's seas of fur. Skeptics questioned whether a single flea could be recognizable, even one as white as Santa's beard. But his colorless abdomen, according to Dr. Ahab, could not be mistaken. And so in time, it was not so much his cunning that distinguished him from other fleas, but his whiteness, the sole characteristic by which he was identified.

His whiteness was appalling, as whiteness is not so much a color as the absence of all colors. Though it generally enhances beauty, as in pearls, doves and wedding gowns, and though a white uniform symbolizes the cleanliness of a waitress, the sterility of a doctor and the purity, avoidance of ego and simplicity of a karate master and, as the painter confronts the infinite potential of the white canvas, something mysterious lurks in all these associations that strikes more panic than the redness of blood.

The elusive quality of the color, especially when coupled with an object that already terrifies, increases that terror ten fold. The milky way scares us with its voids and immensity. The color of the shark and the Ku Klux Klan make them more terrifying than the leopard or tiger. The White Flea symbolized all these things. It was no wonder he was hunted with such fervor.

Dr. Ahab was filled with that fervor. On top of the insect's white abdomen he piled all his rage and hate. Moby represented the evil all men feel eating up their insides until they are left with only half a heart and half a lung. All malice, all malevolence was made assailable in Moby. He was the crawling demon in the hairs of life.

It was true the doctor had hired Kevin and Kit to assist with his search for that demon. With Kit excused from doing so, Kevin's load doubled, and he became quite skilled at discovering and capturing fleas. With a quick flip of his wrist he was able to catch one on his comb then toss it into a bowl of soapy water. Rodney, though a veteran flea searcher, became fascinated by his uncommon artistry. Using his iPhone, he shot a video of Kevin extricating fleas from the black and white hairs of a Boston Terrier then flipping them into the water, including close-up shots of all aspects of the procedure. Rodney considered it a first-rate video with good lighting and angles and, though it lacked sound, posted it on YouTube. Kevin feared this might cause trouble, as it had been shot with neither the dog owner's nor Dr. Ahab's permission. But when Quiznos happened to hear about it from Kit (who was unable to bring himself to view it), she enjoyed watching it. And when she mentioned it to Dr. Ahab, he only asked what YouTube was and when told, wanted to know if the White Flea had been mentioned, which of course, the video having no sound, it had not. Later after some pondering, the doctor appeared in the examination room to announce to Rodney and Kevin, "No more Youtune. We don't want to teach dog owners how to conduct a flea search."

Watching the agony of the tiny insects as they writhed and died in the soapy water began to fill Kevin with uneasiness. Sometimes he felt like a murderer. Even the smallest creatures deserve to live, he thought. The world is made of predators and prey, and fleas should not be punished for instinctively maintaining their role in this balance. And yet I have been watching them die with no remorse.

"Rodney," Kevin said one day as they worked side by side cutting the nails of a medium-sized poodle sporting round fluffs of hair on her ankles, tail and top of her head. "Do insects feel pain?"

This was precisely the kind of question Rodney enjoyed discussing. "No one knows, and how could they? You can't interview a flea, you can't. But there are a lot of theories . . .well not a lot, but quite a few. The most popular is they must feel pain because they run to avoid it. They run, and they struggle to get away, they do. All living organisms, even the flea, try to escape their predators. Pain helps them survive, it does."

"So fleas are intelligent?"

"Have you ever heard a flea give a speech, have you? Have you ever read a book written by a flea? No, fleas aren't smart, not like ants and bees. Ants and bees live in colonies and care for each other, they do. But the flea has only two things to do in life, suck blood and reproduce. He's on his own, he is, and doesn't relate even to other fleas."

"But what about a flea circus? Don't fleas do acrobatics and play musical instruments?"

Rodney gave him a mocking laugh. "You think a flea can play a harp or drive a chariot? The flea circus is one of the most bogus, fraudulent, made-up tricks in the history of entertainment, it is! They used to wire fleas to little props like bass fiddles and carts and heat the floor of the circus, they did. It made the fleas squirm as they tried to escape, so it looked like they were performing, but no. Fleas are useless, good-for-nothing pests, they are. Their only talent is to suck blood. You want to see a real flea circus, do you? Put one on your arm and watch the show!"

Two days later, Kevin met Gabriel, another of Dr. Ahab's workers, a young blond man with pock-marked skin, a blue windbreaker and a deep-set delirium in his eyes. As Kevin was running his flea comb over the long body of a restless dachshund, they conversed, Gabriel revealing he had been working in the clinic for twelve years. Kevin found a number of fleas on the dog's stomach and caught one with his comb.

"You find something?" Gabriel's odd tone of voice seemed a cover-up for a troubled mind.

"Yes." Kevin was about to hurl the bug into his bowl of soapy water when Gabriel said, "And what will you do with that insect?"

"Drown it," Kevin replied.

"Do you really want to make it suffer? Yes, fleas are ugly pests, but they have a right to live just like you or me."

Gabriel patiently listened to Kevin's response. "Last night I read on the PETA website that flea infestations should be judged on a case-by-case basis. It's okay to kill them if they're causing significant suffering to another animal."

"True." Gabriel handed him a glass jar about seven inches high with a metal lid. "And there are some humane insecticides PETA approves of. But if you have the option of saving a flea or killing one, why not save it?"

Kevin stared at the empty jar, then at the flea squirming between the close-set teeth of his comb, its flattened, scaly body and penetrating mouthpiece.

Intent on his mission, Gabriel said, "Drop the fleas into this jar, and before you go home tonight, give it to me, and I'll release them back into nature where they belong."

Later that day a young woman brought a stray mutt to the clinic she had found sleeping near a curb on Palmetto Street. In the past, Quiznos would have immediately directed her to the pound, but since Dr. Ahab's quest had begun, all stray dogs brought to his clinic were first searched for fleas. This dog happened to be hosting quite a number of them. Kevin was dropping them into Gabriel's jar when Dr. Ahab appeared.

"Gabriel caught you?" the doctor said.

"He made a case for animal rights, even for fleas."

"You should have been told. The next time he's here you can conduct your flea searches in the X-ray room."

Dr. Ahab indicated the spray bottles and cans lying on the nearby counter. "Grandma's Homemade Pest Control," one of the labels read. The others had similar sentiments: "Eco-Friendly Insect Control, Made with Natural, Sustainable Ingredients," and "Mom-Approved, Kill with Compassion!"

"These are Gabriel's sprays," Dr. Ahab said. "Useless. They work more to attract fleas than to eliminate them." He went to the other side of the room to open a cabinet there. "We keep the real sprays here." Inside were bottles and cans on whose labels were written harsher promises, presented in red or black uppercase, bold-faced italics that included many exclamation points: "Pestracide Kills!", "Demon Killer Delivers a Quick Knockdown", "Doom! Won't leave a Bug Alive!" and

"Nuke 'Em! Flea and Tick Spray" accompanied by images of skulls and crossbones and pictures of insects lying dead on their backs. "When Gabriel comes in we keep these hidden. Try not to talk to him about fleas. Fortunately, we rarely see him."

By the end of the day, Kevin had collected about thirty fleas in the jar that he presented to Gabriel. Gabriel looked pleased. "You will be placed within the flow of cooperation and congeniality within the universe," he said in his all-knowing voice.

"Quiznos," Kevin said later when he stopped by her desk. "Why does Dr. Ahab allow Gabriel to work for him? They seem at odds with each other, to say the least."

Quiznos always impressed Kevin with her ability to speak even as she typed. "Gabriel is Dr. Ahab's son," she said, keeping her eyes on her computer screen. "Didn't you know?"

Kevin remembered hearing about a son but saw little resemblance.

Quiznos stopped typing and looked up at him. "He began working here years ago. He always seemed lost and aimless but, one day after a trip to Tibet, he came back with a strange look in his eyes and told us he'd joined PETA. His philosophy of saving animals from suffering and murder worked fine in the clinic until the doctor's accident, when all the flea searching started. They've been head to head ever since."

Later in the men's room, Kevin spotted some dark specks in the sink. Upon closer look, they were dead fleas. If these were the same fleas he had dropped into Gabriels' jar, he didn't know.

Though Gabriel's words seemed to make sense, Kevin was still not sure of his position on killing fleas. That evening, after a quick search on the internet, he found some astounding facts, that two thousand species of fleas exist worldwide and that a female flea can lay about fifty eggs at a time and about 2,000 eggs in her lifetime. It seemed the flea population was large enough that the twenty or so fleas he found in a week would not be missed, and he might be playing a necessary predatory role. From then on he had little trouble dropping them into a bowl of soapy water.

That evening he and Weewag engaged in the games they had begun to enjoy, catch and hide the treat. Though the dog continued to amuse and distract him and seemed to be enjoying his new toy, his problem had not been resolved. Kevin's furniture continued to be the victim of the dog's desire to chew, for what reason, Kevin didn't know.

"Weewag, what can I do with you?" he said, wondering where he had put his adoption papers. He once again searched online for solutions to the problem and in the end concluded he needed to be patient. If the dog was anxious as a result of being left alone, in time he would learn to trust that Kevin would always return to him. If not, Kevin didn't know for how long he'd be able to tolerate the behavior.

IX

OFFICE POLITICS

Dr. Ahab may have appeared aloof and ungrateful to his employees, but constantly aware of them, he worked hard to maintain a professional and highly functional office. He was far too decent and honorable a doctor to abandon his medical duties but needed to ease his time in the clinic. He put forth a new rule: he would no longer treat nor take on as new patients cats, ferrets, rabbits or any other small or exotic pet.

He instructed Quiznos to tell callers, "We only treat dogs." A few seconds of silent wonder on the other end of the line usually followed and then, "But I had no idea a veterinarian could do that."

"Yes, it's the thing now," Quiznos would say. "Veterinarians are specializing, just like medical doctors. If your ferret is sick, you find a ferret doctor."

It was important Dr. Ahab examine every dog in town, to lure them to his clinic under any pretense. In treating these dogs, he made a point of displaying the same passionate interest in their well-being he had previously shown. He knew that any neglect of his patients might expose him to the charge of malpractice, and his workers had every right to refuse his orders, quit, or worse, report him to the AVMA. Despite this, he always demanded a flea search, with or without the owner's permission and whether or not an owner reported an excess of scratching.

Dr. Ahab depended on others, and others can be unreliable. He knew whatever power he had over Quiznos had its failings, that she hated his quest and wished he would give it up. She was inclined to fall into open acts of rebellion—plugging her ears with earbuds which cut off all communication with her co-workers, snacking on crunchy chips that echoed like thunder in the doctor's ears and placing Atomic HotBalls in her candy bowl that some pet owners found difficult to tolerate— until he reminded her of her place in the clinic.

The rebellious Quiznos, the reckless Rodney, the nervous Kit, the unreliable Gabriel and the inexperienced Kevin seemed specially chosen by some infernal fatality in the doctor to aid with his revenge. They so exuberantly responded to the old man's anguish that at times his misery seemed theirs, the White Flea as much their foe as his.

But even if Moby incites the hearts of my employees, Dr. Ahab thought, even if he makes them feel like crusaders and they join my chase, they must also have food for their daily appetites. I won't deny them the idea they're helping the sick animals we treat. They look for job satisfaction. What greater reward than to save some poor animal's life? So he tried his best to make sure the hunt was stripped of its rancor and kept in the background. This wasn't difficult, as however eagerly and impetuously his crew stepped up, none of them had lost an eye.

But an eye was not all that Dr. Ahab had lost. All his humor, forced or natural, vanished as well, and he no longer tried to raise a smile. He had always seen laughter as a good thing and hard to come by, and while a veterinarian's job is not always joyful and is sometimes characterized by sickness and woe, in the past, whenever appropriate, he allowed himself a joke or two. But now his dark mood cost him the companionship of his fellow veterinarians. All personal friendships fell by the wayside as well, and when included in group invitations to conventions and gatherings, he made himself alien to them. Like a hermit in a cabin in the woods, he shut himself in his office with no fear of losing himself to inhuman solitudes.

Three weeks after Dr. Ahab's return to the clinic, Rodney, with Kit following, ventured into his office.

"We should all go to the bar, Dr. Ahab. We should," Rodney said, "like we used to. It's six o'clock. Come with us to the Tipsy Horse. We'll buy you a beer, we will."

Dr. Ahab eyed them with near suspicion. "A beer? No. You're too damn jolly."

"Just one beer. You look like you could use one, you do."

"How wondrously familiar is a fool!" Dr. Ahab muttered. "If you feel gay and want to carouse, then call me dark and brooding. Out of my office, please."

X

KEVIN CHASES A WHITE FLEA

Dr. Ahab might have preferred to carouse with a dog. Dogs had the potential to deliver him his foe and set him in a temporary calm. It was the owners who plagued him. One such owner was a Dr. Carey, who, with a coiffed beard and swathed in a bristling shark-skin suit, arrived in the clinic one day leading a Pembroke Welsh Corgi and carrying a thin, leather briefcase. His dog was lethargic, he told Dr. Ahab, and a blood test could likely determine the cause. "I'm a doctor, too," he said as he and Kevin set the small, fluffy dog on the examination table, "though I don't treat animals."

"What kind of doctor?" Kevin asked, trying to fill Dr. Ahab's brooding silence, holding the dog while his employer prepared a syringe.

"A plastic surgeon."

Dr. Ahab stopped his work to face the other doctor. "I suppose you can smooth almost any face, never mind how old, Doctor?"

"Yes, Sir, I think I can, most wrinkles and sags."

"Look here, then." Dr. Ahab put down the syringe and approached Dr. Carey. "Look here. Can you smooth out a crease like this, Doctor?" He swept one hand across his ribbed brow. "If you could, I would be glad to lay my head on your table and feel your slicing and stretching of my skin. Can you smooth this?"

"Oh," Dr. Carey said. "I said I think I can. I said most, but not all."

Dr. Ahab set to finding the dog's vein. "Yes, Doctor. It's the exception," he said. "Unsmoothable. Though you only see it here in my flesh, it has worked down into the bone of my skull—*that* is where the wrinkles lie! But, enough of this nonsense, no more kidding around. Have you seen any fleas on your dog? Any white fleas?"

Dr. Carey revealed his ignorance on the subject. "A white flea? Does such a flea exist?" he said good-humoredly. "I know nothing about fleas. Could they be the cause of her problem?"

Dr. Ahab asked Dr. Carey to sit in the waiting room while he drew the blood, and as soon the other man had gone and a vial was filled, Kevin began combing the dog for fleas. He found nothing on her overlong back or front legs and, after rolling the animal over, no insect appeared in her groin or armpits. But heading over her stomach just to the right of her left front leg was a group of fleas including one that certainly seemed to lack color. He grabbed the white tufts of fur around it to improve his view of it, to eye the beauty of its tiny, milky body as it shifted and glistened in the sunlight that streamed through the window. Excitement surged through him.

"The White Flea—the White Flea!"

"Quiet!" Dr. Ahab said. "Don't burst a blood vessel. Whisper only!" He approached the dog and bent over to peer at its belly. "Get the Pest Police."

Hearts beating, in a rush of feverish anticipation, both retrieved their spray cans and held them ready. The Corgi gave a slow and laborious inhalation. The flea emerged from the hairs at the base of her right front leg.

"Follow it, follow it," Dr. Ahab said, his eye clear and alive, "but keep cool, easy. Don't raise the dead from their graves." The tiny monster flitted its rear segment and sank out of sight, but farther up the dog's lower abdomen it rose again, full speed ahead. Kevin began to count on the honor of the capture. The dog's poor stub of a tail beat as if in agony or fright.

"Shoot!" Dr. Ahab commanded.

Kevin pushed hard on his can's nozzle until blinding gusts of white vapor filled the air. While waiting for the fog to clear, he pictured the insect writhing and twisting in agony, not far from reality. It sat on the dog's stomach spasming from side to side until finally, having succumbed to the boiling spray, it lay motionless.

The doctor bent over the dog to give the flea a closer look. "It's not him," he finally said. "It's just the sun that makes him look white."

Kevin stood, thoughtfully eyeing the tiny corpse it made. It was indeed brown, he regretfully acknowledged. But in those few seconds of sighting and spraying, in his single-mindedness to kill, he had learned the joy of the hunt, the exhilaration, the rapture. His commitment was sealed. This flea was not Moby, but the next one would be.

XI

THE SPREADSHEET

In the solitude of his office, Dr. Ahab often paced from his desk to his door and back again, then paused before his iMac. There, his one eye would stare fixedly on its screen, on a file labeled "Dog Log." He would then resume his walk, then pause before his desk again and give the file another glance, this one dashed with a wild longing, if not hopefulness. He would then sit to contemplate this log, adding and deleting the names of dogs and their owners listed. Often the sun shone through his office window, throwing shifting gleams and shadows upon his wrinkled brow. While he typed, invisible hands typed too, on the deeply marked chart of his forehead.

Though contact tracing was no longer an option, there was still hope in searching for Moby on every dog in town. Of the two hundred twenty-seven neighborhood dogs the doctor could account for, many remained unknown to him. He was constantly updating and familiarizing his crew with those already on his list. He had hired Kevin and Kit to help in his clinic and, when time permitted, to visit the local dog park, to document the dogs that played there and try to lure them to his office. Kit had set up the "Dog Log" and showed Dr. Ahab how to add or delete text and photos. Modern technology, once a mystery to the doctor's rigid mind, was now in part solved thanks to Kit and to his own determination to defeat Moby.

Dr. Ahab also asked the owners of Howlistic and Animal

House to reveal the names of the pet owners who came in to purchase flea powders, sprays or collars. In exchange he would recommend their stores to his patients. Neither store owner was aware the doctor was recommending both at the same time and saw no superiority of one over the other.

The spreadsheet's first heading, "Inspected," included the names of each dog already searched and on which date. The next, "To be Inspected" included three subheadings: "Nanford Dog Park" included photos of unfamiliar dogs seen at the local park needing to be identified, "Patients" listed the names of the dogs treated in his clinic in the past he had not yet checked for fleas and "Flea Product Purchasers" included the name, address and phone number of recent purchasers of flea sprays, ointments or collars in the two local pet stores. The latter two lists were updated daily, and any newly acquired phone numbers were submitted to Quiznos who continued to use them until direct contact was made with the dog owners, when she would offer a free flea search.

Though Dr. Ahab put much faith in his spreadsheet, he was as ignorant of the potential of the computer as he was well-versed in animal medicine. He asked Rodney the conspirer to invent schemes to increase his business (and thereby his potential to find Moby) then had Kit create the graphics. Their first collaboration, "Free Flea Inspection For Your Dog, No Scratching Does Not Mean No Fleas. Call for a House Call," first displayed in the *Nanford Banner*, was then emailed to all the dog owners on the doctor's list. About half called to make an appointment, though more seemed motivated by the desire to receive something for nothing than concern over their pet. Rodney would make house calls to those who requested one, but after a week of such visits, those dogs with fleas were not harboring a white one, while most hosted no fleas at all. When he roamed the neighborhood with a comb and a bottle of soapy water offering a free search to any dog walker he came across, he received a variety of reactions:

"There are plenty of YouTube videos on how to search for fleas."

"We're a very clean household, thank you."

"Who do you work for, the government?"

With his long hair and alien ears, Rodney had few takers, and this option was soon put on hold.

On a sunny Saturday afternoon in April, the dog park was as populated as the streets of old Delhi, and served as a virtual haven for fleas. Martha, Roxy, Zelda, Harley, Luna, Boomer, and Dixie were among the dogs Dr. Ahab hoped to lure, the ones seen there every day, those spry enough to run up and down apartment building stairs, able to leap high in the air to catch a ball, who sped in a blur past Kevin, Kit and Rodney, whose hearts beat with the vitality of an Olympian athlete, who had no reason to step a paw into Dr. Ahab's clinic.

Not every owner took his dog to the park, but most dogs there were local. The three employees visited it alone or in pairs and recorded the names of unfamiliar dogs when called to or scolded by their owners. If an unidentified dog was leaving the park, one of them secretly followed it home, noted its address, perhaps got a name off a mailbox, then searched online for contact information for its owner.

When no owner brought his dog to the clinic for grooming, dental problems, vaccinations or any other ailment, Dr. Ahab was at the mercy of the illnesses that might strike a dog but stopped short of coming up with a plan to spread some mild disease throughout the area. He was fighting against time and forced to set his quest in emergency mode. The object of his pursuit might be long dead or dying.

"Have I not figured him out yet?" Dr. Ahab muttered to himself one late evening after poring over his spreadsheet. "Have I studied him just to let him escape?" What torment the doctor endured, consumed by this unrelenting desire for revenge! His mad mind raced until a weariness overtook him, and to recover his strength, he left the clinic to walk Nanford's desolate streets. Back in his office, he napped in his armchair with clenched fingers. As he slept, dreams whirled in his brain until it throbbed with anguish, and a chasm seemed to open inside him from which flames shot up. A wild cry echoed throughout the clinic and, with glaring eyes, Dr. Ahab burst from his office as though escaping a bed on fire.

XII

A PRANK

Within the clinic, nothing was said or done without the subtext of the search. When all the people existing in one place serve an emotional man, that emotion rules, if not by words then by every glance, every gesture.

Flea or no flea, between his employees persisted a tacit competition for the old man's approval. Like machines, they dumbly moved about, always conscious of the doctor's despotic eye. As laughter is contagious, so is woe. And when the boss is moody, the employees feel responsible for that moodiness. A challenge is presented—to commit some deed to rouse his spirits and lighten his gloom. Dr. Ahab was the unloving parent of children seeking to please him. It went further than mere searching for fleas. It meant scheming and inventing.

Kevin wasn't sure what he thought of Rodney's attempt to cause a flea infestation in the dog park. He understood the motivation to please his boss, but he also knew of Rodney's love of animals. Rodney himself was not one to ask. He seemed close-mouthed on the subject. He was late to meet Kevin at the park and tried to change the subject when Kevin observed the excessive amount of scratching there.

"It's flea season? Yes, it must be." Rodney lifted his phone and spent some time aiming it at a nearby Chihuahua. He was trying to make himself look busy taking pictures of the unfamiliar dogs but appeared to be shooting any dog that passed.

Scoping out the dog park was always pleasant work, especially in April. The sky was clear except for a few low-hanging clouds strangely shaped by pollutants. Despite Nanford's concrete terrain, spring was able to announce itself, if not with budding or flowering, at least with rising temperatures. They watched dogs of all ages, colors, sizes and breeds playing, barking and relieving themselves. There were blind and deaf dogs, limping dogs, osteoporotic dogs, dogs attached to wheels, sleeping dogs, humping dogs, dogs who stood on their hind legs and dogs who chased balls and caught frisbees. There were leaders, followers, cliques of dogs, jealous dogs, flirtatious dogs, dogs who would not play, unfriendly dogs, scared dogs, dogs looking to pick a fight, dogs with no concept of their size, dogs who sat with their owners and dogs who pulled on their leashes, refusing to leave the park. In that park was a microcosm of society.

"That Chihuahua reminds me of Natasha, she does," Rodney said. "She has that same deer head and the same stand-up ears. Natasha could speak, did I tell you? She could sing, too. Her favorite song was Ebb Tide, it was."

Kevin assumed this reminiscence was a ploy to distract him, but the misty look in Rodney's eyes seemed genuine. Kevin didn't mean to be critical. His motivation was more curiosity than accusation, a need to affirm the extent of Rodney's loyalty to the doctor, a possible example to follow. "What was it you had to do before you met me here?" Kevin said.

Rodney's lack of response was most likely the silence of guilt, Kevin thought. Although both had worked at the clinic all morning, Rodney had insisted they walk separately to the park as he needed to attend to something beforehand. It did not take a Columbo to deduce Rodney's scheme. Kevin was tired of being polite. "You really want to jeopardize the health of all these dogs?" he said.

Rodney's camera followed a passing Afghan Hound. His incentive was obvious, but if the planted fleas came directly from the clinic, his plan made no sense. He would simply be returning the fleas to where they had come from.

He shrugged and avoided Kevin's eyes. "It wasn't that many fleas, only four or five per dog. There are worse conditions than having fleas, there are. There are ear infections, worms, dermatitis . . ."

But as the result of Rodney's scheme, the number of Dr. Ahab's clients did not increase. Kevin realized that most pet owners did not consider a few fleas a dire condition, and if they did, a wide variety of websites and the clerks in the two local pet stores could provide plenty of advice and information on how to eliminate them. An experienced veterinarian was not required to fix the problem. And most importantly, Rodney had not been able to write Dr. Ahab's phone number on the back of each flea.

After spending the day with an employer who rarely gave him encouragement or thanks for his hard work, Kevin was grateful for the love and affection at home. For a while now, he was returning there to find nothing torn or shredded, no upsets but what he had left amiss himself. Weewag had somehow found inner peace and was proving to be an ideal housemate, considerate of Kevin's moods and licking his floors clean. Now at last, the dog trusted that Kevin would always come back to him, and the bond that should have been sealed long ago was beginning to blossom.

XIII

A NEW FRIEND

The next time Kevin visited the park, not a dog was scratching, and not one dog vest, sweater, bandana or bootie remained. The cloudless sky looked brilliantly lacquered, and the June sun blazed with a radiance so insufferable he had no choice but to put on his Ray-Bans. He and Weewag had walked treeless streets on their way, passing fast food drive-ins baking in the sun, cars of the lightest colors wearing sunshades, and drugstore windows displaying bottles of sun block of the highest SPF numbers. Owners and their dog overtook the sidewalks, and they joined them taking in the sights, sounds and smells at their different perspectives, by the different capabilities of their senses, each with his own level of appreciation.

Inside the park Kevin sat on a bench and watched Weewag run with a medium sized pug showing more interest in him than he showed in it. My dog is popular, Kevin thought. He's always a little aloof and keeps an air of mystery about him that attracts other dogs. Kevin spotted an unfamiliar Labrador Retriever, waited for him to come near and took his picture. The discovery of a new neighborhood dog would be quite a coup to Dr. Ahab. He would delight in seeing the photo, and in the deep black hairs of the dog's sleek coat, Kevin imagined a multitude of fleas.

"Black dogs are hard to photograph," came a sweet voice from the next bench over. He turned to see a young woman facing him. She wore thick-lensed, dark-rimmed glasses that lent an air of depth and intelligence to her merely pretty face, glasses appearing so heavy he wondered if her delicate-looking nose might at any moment collapse underneath them. He wondered too if, judging by the rosiness of her skin and the intensity of the colors she wore, some hidden fortitude lay inside her. The glasses made her appear bookish, but perhaps were only correctional. It soon became obvious the former was the case. "Big, black dogs are the least likely to be adopted from animal shelters. They even have a name for it, Big Black Dog syndrome or BBD. People would rather adopt light-colored dogs. There are a few theories as to why. One is that black dogs are often portrayed as evil or aggressive on TV or in the movies. Also, there's that superstition about black cats that they transfer to dogs. And of course, they're harder to photograph." Her cheeks flushed with the same red color as the McDonald's sign in the distance behind her. "Which one is yours?"

Weewag, now away from the others, stood in the middle of the park sniffing the base of the one tree that had managed to grow there. Kevin pointed him out, told her the dog's name and that he had just adopted him.

"I'm Charity. I work at the library. You're Kevin, right?"

Kevin found it hard to believe he did not remember her, that he had not made a mental note of an attractive female he had allegedly come across. He wondered if his pessimism concerning relationships with women had removed the part of his brain that noticed them, in an unconscious attempt at self-preservation, and his eyes had been shielded by foggy lenses. But there was no reason to be concerned. He had recently become a little more dog-oriented, that was all. He sometimes noticed himself judging dogs the same way he used to judge women, assessing their faces, their legs and their tail ends, looking at their proportions and the way they held themselves. He could have described Weewag with his eyes closed. At least he was still discerning of an animal, if not one of his own species. It was simply a slight shift in interest that he could easily return to under the right circumstances.

"So how are you two getting along?" Charity said. "Good chemistry between a dog and a person can be just as hard to find as between two people."

"Weewag and I are doing just fine." He wondered if beneath his tone lay the words, "so please stay away," but this wasn't his desire. Here was a chance to spend some pleasurable time with a new person. "Which dog is yours?"

She cupped her hands over her mouth and let out a shout of unexpected force and volume. "Stella!" A medium-sized bulldog unfamiliar to Kevin trotted towards them. A few black spots marred her otherwise silvery coat.

"Stella's an English bulldog," Charity said as the dog jumped onto the bench beside her. She pet the dog's head. "Aren't you, sweetie?"

"Are you here on your lunch break?" Kevin said.

"Yes," she said, as the dog lay quietly. "You?"

"Yes. I work for a veterinarian here in Nanford."

"You own a dog, take your lunch break in a dog park, work for a veterinarian and take pictures of dogs. You must really love dogs."

"I do."

While they talked of other things, Stella remained with them, and Kevin took a picture of her which Charity oohed and aahed at and insisted it was one of the most flattering ever taken of her. "You caught her best angle," she said. "Will you send it to me?" She gave him her email address.

Charity's brain, it turned out, was brimming with information on almost any topic. It was as if while sitting in the library surrounded by books for the past three years, she had by osmosis taken in all their contents. Their conversation proceeded from heroes of Celtic mythology to the science behind Montessori to the history of the Basques from Roman rule to the present. Fortunately, Kevin was an avid reader himself and nearly able to keep up with her. But after a good half-hour of non- veterinarian topics, realizing there was little time left on his lunch hour, he knew he had to quickly steer the conversation to the subject of fleas. While they conversed, he had noted a few unfamiliar dogs and had taken their pictures. A brand new specimen lay practically by his side, and he wasn't about to lose the opportunity to inspect her. Despite the pleasant distraction Charity provided, he would not abandon the reason for his presence in the park.

He tried to reconsider. Why ruin a perfectly good exchange in order to please a crazy veterinarian? He should have been able to enjoy the warm weather, the gentle wind playing at the dog's ears and the few green leaves fluttering on the tree. But when they'd completely exhausted the topic of air-conditioning in Japan, he couldn't help but blurt, "So, does Stella have fleas?" He could hardly believe the silly non sequitur had come out of his mouth.

Charity looked appropriately perplexed and hesitated at this abrupt left turn in the heretofore smooth flow of their conversation. "Not that I know of. Why? I mean, she doesn't scratch herself. Wouldn't that mean she doesn't?"

"Not necessarily. I'm not a vet, but in my experience, a dog might not scratch and still have them. Does she have hair loss? Pale gums?"

"She loses a little hair now and then. But I thought that was normal. And I've never looked at her gums, but—"

"If you like, I could give you a free flea search."

Her pretty green eyes almost crossed. "Now?"

"Sure, why not?"

"Now you have me worried."

"It would only take a minute."

"What's in it for you?"

"The vet I work for has concern for all dogs."

Stella had by this time run off to flirt with a shepherd-like mutt about her size. They were sniffing each other when Charity beckoned Stella with another ear-splitting yell. Judging by her funny waddle and the determined look on her flat face, Kevin wondered if the name Stella was meant to be ironic. But though he found her unappealing, her coat, shiny and unblemished, couldn't have looked cleaner, and her gums were a robust red. In fact, Kevin had never seen a healthier dog. Even before he removed the fine-toothed comb and paper towel folded in quarters from his pocket, he was sure he would not find a single flea on her.

XIV

QUIZNOS WRESTLES WITH HER CONSCIENCE

The poor dogs of Nanford, the sorry victims of the doctor's heated quest, who stood patiently while poked and probed. Dr. Ahab now viewed them as coconspirators with Moby, as if they had signed a pact with him to hide him in their fur. But in exchange for what? There would be no benefit but itchy, blotchy skin.

Wednesday morning at nine a.m., a young woman entered the clinic accompanied by a stubby, black Rottweiler named Dash with an appointment to be neutered. She arranged to pick him up at six, allowing the appropriate number of hours for his recovery. In the surgery room, Rodney gave Dash a sedative, Kit weighed him and Kevin set up the surgery tools. After Rodney cleaned and disinfected the area on the dog to be incised, positioned him on the table and covered him with a light blanket, Kit called in Dr. Ahab. The doctor placed a tube down the dog's windpipe to deliver the anesthesia then successfully performed the operation, sutured the incision and turned off the gas. But the poor dog, after ten minutes, showed no signs of waking.

"Give him some time. Knock on my door when he comes to," the doctor said, washing his hands. "Let me know if he goes into convulsions." He retired to his office.

His crew looked at each other in horror. Shouldn't the doctor keep watch? They resumed the clean-up, never far from the dog's side.

Quiznos came into the room. "Any change yet?"

"Not yet," Rodney said. "What do your cards say?"

Quiznos left the room, went to her desk, opened its top drawer and took out her deck of tarot cards. As receptionist, she answered the phone, scheduled and re-scheduled appointments, sent out bills, balanced the books and sometimes lent what veterinary skills she had picked up over the years to treating animals. In addition, she was an accomplished reader of tarot cards. She cleared her desk and laid out three cards in a row which she repeated three times. She exhaled with relief. No cards associate with death appeared, and two represented healing.

She hurried back to the surgery room. "The dog will live," she announced, and all breathed easier. Three minutes later the dog's torso wriggled a little, then he moved his head. Soon he was awake, eyes open, breathing normally. His tail gave one weak wag. All cheered, and Quiznos headed down the hall to inform Dr. Ahab. But before knocking on his closed door, she paused. His office was generally off-limits. The hallway light, about to burn out, cast fitful shadows on the door, its window covered by a Venetian blind. She stood in silence, far from the examination room chatter.

The last time I sided against him, she thought, he looked about to murder me. I've come to tell him the dog's revived, but it's really the revival of that damn insect. And he'll search for it right away, never mind the dog's condition. The Veterinarian's Oath wouldn't allow a flea search right now. The dog needs rest. He's vulnerable to infection and might feel sick from the anesthesia. But Dr. Ahab would fire me or anyone else who went against him. I need to convince him he's wrong and take away his power. He only wants me to do what he wants. He claims everyone else does, that we're all Ahabs.

If I report him to the AVMA, every vet in the area will find out, and the guilt would be too much. I wouldn't be able to live with myself. Even if I could make my case, the crazy doctor would drag all us loyal employees down with him and we'd all be out of a job. But here's my chance to prevent all this.

But I'm being silly, she thought. Dr. Ahab's conducted dozens of flea searches before and he hasn't hurt a single dog. She raised her fist preparing to knock, but then slowly lowered it.

But no, she thought. The dog might suffer for it and it'll be on my conscience. What was that? I think I hear him muttering in his sleep, as if he heard my thoughts.

"Back away everyone!" she heard. "Moby, come out and face your death!"

She turned from the door and walked back to the examination room to speak to the rest. "He's sound asleep. Somebody else should tell him."

XV

AN OUTING

When Kevin received an email from Charity asking if he would like to meet her the next evening in the dog park, he hesitated before responding. After his breakup with Amanda, he felt eager to replace her, but after failing to do so, the joy and fulfillment he was receiving from his dog rid him of that notion. He had gotten so used to life without a human mate that the idea of spending time with a potential one now felt regressive, like an old game he used to play that could only end badly. He was a new, evolved person, a rock and an island, and he was beginning to like it that way. But in her invitation, Charity was including their dogs, and as she didn't specify the pairing, he would choose Weewag for himself and enjoy the evening.

The day was grey, not uncommon in a town whose hues ran from taupe to gunmetal, where the tallest buildings were barely distinguishable against an overcast sky. Though dressed in beige and with her warm brown hair, sitting on one of the park's wooden benches, Charity appeared bright and colorful. The lateness of the day had no bearing on the park's popularity. The cooling night air only meant less panting and more energy to devote to running. After Kevin sat next to her, while watching their dogs play, their conversation turned to the subject of their travels. She had seen Wombats in Tasmania, braved a lion sniffing at her tent in the Kenyan wilderness, visited the Dracula castle in Transylvania and spent a summer fishing in Antarctica. He had spent his entire life in Nanford and its immediate surroundings and had been to Toronto a few times to see his sister, he told her, feeling slightly dull.

Their pets socialized with different groups until both raced with a Siberian Husky, but after slowing to a stop and drawing close, they barely sniffed at each other. And even after Kevin and Charity left the park and were walking down Wapping Street, the two dogs seemed to be pulling on their leashes in opposite directions.

"They're barely noticing each other," Kevin said.

"Dogs don't usually look each other in the eye the way we do," Charity said. "They like to show each other their profiles."

"That would be odd if that's all we did." Kevin tried to walk sideways while looking ahead, showing Charity his profile, making Charity laugh.

There was little to do or see in a town so devoid of culture. They walked the sidewalks of the least trafficked streets where a few trees struggled to grow out of fissures in the concrete. "This street is nearly a forest," Kevin joked as they passed two sickly-looking elms. At one point when they stopped at a traffic light, Weewag lay down.

"This is an odd time for a rest, Weewag," Kevin said.

"He's just showing Stella he's giving her the upper hand," Charity said. "And you see how Stella seems disinterested? That's her way of telling him she's going along with it."

"So she's the dominant one?"

"Don't worry. She's not too bossy."

The subject of dominance brought Dr. Ahab to mind. Kevin was not sure how much he wanted to reveal about him, if anything at all. The world of the doctor seemed distant now, the craziness of the search enhanced by its comparison to this slightly odd, but mostly normal outing. He didn't want to spoil it, walking Nanford's barren streets with this interesting young woman. Eventually, though, Kevin had to face it. He felt a strong desire to go home where he and Weewag could spend time doing nothing in particular.

They reached Plymouth Street, a street lined with multi-family houses painted similarly grey. They passed a bright red for sale sign and an assortment of green trash bags that added more gaiety to the street than intended. Four families lived in Charity's house, each distinguished by a window box of a variety of ailing plants. Stopping at her front steps, Charity surveyed the two dogs, Stella sitting contentedly by her legs and Weewag sniffing the sidewalk. "You may be right," she said. "I'm not sure Stella and Weewag like each other."

"Was this a night out for us or our dogs?" Kevin said.

Charity emitted a bell-like laugh, gave him a quick "good-bye, Kevin," and she and Stella headed up the steps.

Walking home he couldn't help noticing a questioning look in Weewag's eyes, as if some unknown threat was about to upset their peaceful coexistence.

"Don't worry, Weewag," he said, wondering if he were imposing his own emotions on his dog's expression.

Monday morning at the clinic, as he combed a fat Basset Hound searching for fleas, he found himself digging more deeply than usual into the dog's fur.

XVI

DR. ENGLISH

Now during the days, Dr. Ahab began to dread the terrors and torments of the night. More often than not, he lay restless and sleepless into the early hours of the morning, his blood rushing in time to the ticking of his clock, plagued by thoughts of his unceasing quest. Even the sheep he counted would eventually turn into small brown bugs, endless processions of them passing through his mind's eye, none of them white. Sometimes, abandoning all hope of rest, he would leave his bed to find comfort within the walls of his clinic, arriving there hours before it was due to open, to sit at his office desk studying his spreadsheet, contemplating, prioritizing and rearranging its contents.

Early Tuesday morning a few minutes before eight, while alphabetizing the most elusive dogs on his list, he heard a knock on the clinic door and chose to ignore it. But seconds later the knock sounded again, this time louder and more insistent. Dr. Ahab closed his file, went to the door and soon found himself face to face with Dr. English, a fellow veterinarian he had met in medical school, a darkly-tanned, burly, good-natured man in his sixties.

Like many others, Dr. English hid his amazement at Dr. Ahab's changed, haggard appearance. Though it seemed his former friend was not going to invite him inside, he spoke in his most amiable manner. "Ahab," he said, "I was concerned about you. I've been trying to get in touch with you, but you won't return my calls."

"I've been lately occupied with this or that." Dr. Ahab was still not stepping aside to let him in.

"So I thought I'd drop by before your workday."

"So you did. For what reason? Have you seen the White Flea?"

Dr. English hid his dismay at the question that seemed to confirm rumors concerning the sanity of his fellow veterinarian. "I gave up my practice. May I come in?"

Eager to return to his files, Dr. Ahab quickly ushered Dr. English into his waiting room. "Did you?"

Dr. English pulled up his left sleeve to reveal his forearm where a large, crusty, red and green wound in the shape of Florida was still healing. In less than a few seconds, Dr. Ahab was leading his guest into his office, but in the excitement of the moment and because of the new limitations on his visual field, he incorrectly judged the opening of his door and knocked his acquaintance on the right side of his head. This awkwardness lasted only a few seconds, soon all was forgiven and they were sitting across from each other at the doctor's desk.

"When did it happen? Was it a flea?" Dr. Ahab said.

"It was two weeks ago."

"And he bit you, did he?"

"Yes. Just like you were bit."

"Tell me, was it Moby?" Dr. Ahab inched to the edge of his seat and leaned towards him.

"I believe it was. I was treating my first patient of the day, a tricolored mutt, mostly Bernese Mountain Dog. She had been scratching something awful, the owner told me. I searched her fur, especially around the base of her tail. There I found a cluster of fleas, including one the color of which in all my years as a vet, I had never seen before."

"It was white?"

"And insecticide decorating its back."

"Yes, that's Moby," Dr. Ahab said, his one revealed eye gleaming. "Go on! Did you kill him? What became of him?"

"Give me a chance," Dr. English said good-humoredly, rubbing the side of his head. "Remembering your encounter, terror seized me, but I was determined to attack him before he attacked me. But as soon as he sensed me there, this colorless flea jumped onto my arm and went to snapping furiously at it."

Dr. Ahab nodded. "Yes, he sensed the nearby host. Jump and bite. That's Moby! I know him. Go on!"

"How it was exactly," continued the injured veterinarian, "I don't know. But in biting me, his foul mouth got caught in my skin, so when I pulled on him, the barb ripped its way along my flesh, clear down my arm. He stuck tight and drank deep until my skin turned red and swollen. Despite his boiling rage, hoping to unhinge him, I hit him with a shower of Imidacloprid, which completely fogged my eyes. I could barely see the flea bursting off me and back onto the dog.

"Blood dripped down my arm," Dr. English went on, "so I disinfected it, then I bandaged it. It kept getting worse until it turned black. I was afraid I'd need an amputation. My doctor was shocked at the sight of it. He prescribed an antibiotic ointment, kept a close watch on it, and it healed, thank God. My doctor was strict, but trustworthy. I'd rather be killed by him than kept alive by any other man."

Dr. Ahab had been listening to his colleague's discourse with some impatience. "What about the flea? What became of the White Flea?"

"Oh," the other doctor said, "Yes. I have no idea what happened to him, but—"

"Didn't you look for him?"

"No, I didn't look. Isn't one gash enough? What would I do with another ugly scar? Should I lose my eye like you? I don't prefer to go through life flea-bitten! It must be said, Ahab, that what you take for the White Flea's malice is only his awkwardness. He never means to swallow a single human cell. He only wants to terrify you! No, thank you, he's welcome to the blood he already took from me and not a drop more. No flea searching for me. There would have been great glory in killing him, but he's best left alone, don't you think?" His eyes followed upward the path of the thin, black strap that held the eyepatch to the doctor's head as it seemed to cut into his flesh.

His gloomy expression restored, Dr. Ahab leaned back in his chair and fell into deep reflection on the elusiveness of his foe. "I don't agree," he said at last. "I won't give up the hunt. The damn insect consumes me."

"My God," Dr. English said. "Your blood pressure must be rising as we speak. I can practically hear your pulse beat."

But then Dr. Ahab revived and drew himself upright again. "Who owns the dog who hosted the flea and how can I reach him—the mutt that resembles a Bernese Mountain Dog?"

Dr. English shook his head. "I won't tell you, Ahab. You should cease and desist."

"The name of the owner, Dr. English." His tone was commanding.

"If you value your sanity," Dr. English said, "you should put a stop to this at once. It's eating you alive. It may cost you your life. I'm afraid it may already be too late."

Though the visit from his injured colleague did not end well, it did serve to restore hope and renew the doctor's fervor. If Moby was responsible for the attack, and it had occurred only two weeks before, chances were the White Flea was alive and well and still living on the tricolored mutt. It was imperative to find out the name of the owner, and though Dr. English refused to reveal it, his receptionist might not. But he was not familiar with the doctor's former staff. As soon as his friend left the clinic, Dr. Ahab sat once again before his iMac and stared at its screen imagining the infiniteness of the information that lay behind its unblinking stare. His one eye followed the row of tiny multicolored pictures that ran up and down its left side. One of them would surely lead him to the information he sought, but not knowing which, he felt helpless and diminished. He was reluctant to involve his crew in this current dilemma and further reveal the breadth of his obsession, but no other option occurred to him. It was eight fifteen. They would arrive at nine.

The forty-five minute wait proved long and painful. With every passing minute, Moby retreated further from him. Dr. Ahab's inability to confide in a solitary soul the urgency he felt wreaked havoc on his nerves. He spent the time in frenetic pacing, then tried to relax in his chair, only to hoist himself out of it to peer out his window and scan the streets for his incoming workers. He stood by his office door and listened as they drifted in at varying minutes after nine. For them, this was only another humdrum Tuesday morning when, between sips of coffee, pleasantries about the weather and the previous night's activities would be exchanged. As soon as he detected the soft footsteps of Kit about to pass, he opened his door and ordered him inside.

"You still making those pictures?" he asked his apprehensive employee. He had once seen Kit sketching in a drawing pad.

"If you mean drawings, yes," Kit said bashfully, hoping the doctor would remember he'd been drawing during his lunch hour.

"And you like to draw people?"

"Sometimes."

"You can make a drawing of an old man like me?"

"I never did, but I'm sure I could."

"We'll see then, we'll see."

Kit, not sure of the reason for his presence in the office, half turned to leave when Dr. Ahab added, "By the way, I need the name and phone number of Dr. English's receptionist. Dr. English, a veterinarian on Wapping Street. His business is terminated, but see if you can find her."

Vaguely let down that this visit had little or nothing to do with any interest Dr. Ahab may have taken in his artistic abilities, Kit left the office and sat at the employee room iMac. It took him only fifteen minutes to track the receptionist down. It would have taken half that time had he not been distracted by two Facebook notifications of gallery events in Tilsbury, then a friend request from an ex-girlfriend from high school he felt the urgency to accept. After a quick look at his ex's Facebook page that revealed she was still unmarried, he found via Google that Dr. English's clinic website remained on view and included the name of his ex-receptionist, Rachel Gardiner. He then returned to Facebook to see if Rachel had posted a page there, but after finding she had, couldn't help clicking on an ad sitting on its right side promising a way to earn three hundred dollars a week without getting out of bed. After quickly perusing the ad, he returned to Rachel's information and was glad to discover she had included her phone number.

"I used Google and Facebook," he told the doctor after knocking timidly on his office door, not sure if he would understand but hoping this knowledge might assist in any future endeavors. But Dr. Ahab was too pleased with the information to be bothered with how it had been obtained. He ushered Kit out of his office, then phoned Rachel, pushing every necessary phone button with the thrill that came with honing in on his foe.

"Sorry, Dr. Ahab," she said, disappointed the caller had not been her headhunter, "I dealt with a lot of patients, I have no memory for numbers and no access to Dr. English's files."

The doctor, once again in the throes of defeat, was about to hang up when she said, "But I do remember the dog was owned by a Rose Bouton who lives somewhere on Maple Street—"

Dr. Ahab gave a grunt with a gracious ring to it, abruptly hung up, turned to his iMac and once more stared at the screen, taking great effort to remember Kit's words about searching for someone. He recalled the word 'google' and, while once again checking the little pictures on the left side of his screen, finally spotted one with a capital G on it. He clicked on it, and an empty box appeared where he could insert a name. With his right index finger, he was typing letter by letter R O S E when he heard a knock on his door.

"Who's there?" Dr. Ahab continued to type. "Go away!"

"Doctor, it's me, Quiznos."

"Go away, Quiznos."

"A Mrs. Schultz just brought in Rosebud, her Weimaraner. She says it's an emergency. The dog's leg is cut, and it won't stop bleeding. The bandage is leaking. I think you should look at it right away."

"I said please go away."

"Doctor? I'm coming in." Quiznos opened the door to find Dr. Ahab staring at his computer screen, his brow in creases as the list of websites for a multitude of Rose Boutons was appearing.

"A little leakage is normal," he said, without looking at her. "Now I would like to be left alone."

"The dog's licking the bandage so hard it may come loose, Doctor."

"So it will, so it will."

"I'm talking about a Weimaraner, sir."

"And I was not speaking or thinking of one." He glanced at Quiznos as she stood in the doorway, brow furrowed, beaded earrings swaying. "Go away, Quiznos! Let it leak! I'm leaky myself. My leaks are leaking. Yet I don't stop to plug them—"

"And what will the owner say?"

"Let the owner stand outside the building and yell about it. What do I care? Owners, owners! You're always prattling, Quiznos, about those overprotective owners, as if the owners are my conscience. The only real owner of this clinic is me. It is I who dictates what goes on here and no one else!"

Quiznos had long been waiting for an opportunity to speak her mind, and now seemed the perfect moment. She took a deep breath and broke into her long-rehearsed speech.

"Doctor," she said in the calmest manner possible, "I understand what you must be going through. You spend your days treating sick animals. You develop feelings for these animals, and then they may die. I know this is stressful. And as the head of this clinic, you have to hide your feelings. I understand, Doctor! But did you know that in the last thirty years, veterinarians committed suicide almost three times more often than the national average, and that one in six veterinarians has considered it?"

Dr. Ahab stared at her as if she were speaking a different language.

"But there's help. The Tilsbury Veterinary Medical Association sponsors groups for medical people just like you. They teach you meditation, they help you improve your diet, they give you social and behavioral theories. Only a mile away. I can show you the brochure."

But though Dr. Ahab's eye was aimed directly at her, she detected a pull between it and his iMac screen. "Dr. Ahab?"

He finally turned to the screen, then spoke in a voice low and measured. "Thank you, Quiznos," he said. "When I need assistance, I'll let you know."

"Okay, then," she said, before leaving the room. "I've spoken my piece."

Dr. Ahab tried to refocus on the list of Rose Boutons, but now it was Quiznos occupying his thoughts. What did she say? he said to himself. Hmmmm. He got up and again paced the small room, but this time with slower and more deliberate steps. There's a flash of honesty in her, he thought, a prudence that forbids her to speak her real mind. I won't heed her words, but they were hard to come by. And she meant well. The creases in his forehead relaxed, he left his office and went to her desk.

"You're a good woman, Quiznos," he said. "Is the dog still here? Let's take a look at those bandages."

XVII

DETECTIVE WORK

He found Rose Bouton the dermatologist, a filmmaker named Rose Bouton, Rose Bouton the creative director and Rose Bouton the biotechnologist. Dr. Ahab clicked on each link, but discovered no personal information, no mention of any pet dog.

He resignedly pressed on his intercom lever and called Kit back into his office. Kit discovered Rose's phone number in no time, via Facebook. She had included in her photos a picture of Muffin, her small, tricolored mutt. He would have immediately conveyed this information to his employer had he not taken time to confirm three friend requests and peruse a fake news story about Dwayne Johnson that appeared on the right side of Rose's page.

Dr. Ahab submitted the phone number to Quiznos. "This woman's dog was hosting a flea that bit Dr. English on the arm and caused him to close his practice," he told her. "We need to check the dog for fleas. Call her and tell her Dr. English requested I see her for a follow-up visit, that her dog might continue to host fleas. Tell her we won't charge her. Make an appointment at her earliest convenience—if not today then tomorrow. And give her priority."

Quiznos did as she was told. Rose, a part-time accountant, after recovering from her disappointment that Quiznos didn't require help with her tax return, tearfully revealed her awareness of her role in the termination of her veterinarian's practice while the sympathetic Quiznos tried her best to counsel her. More than eager to rid her dog of any residual parasites, Rose hoped during a visit with Dr. Ahab no flea found on Muffin would give a repeat performance. After Quiznos assured her of that unlikeliness, Rose confessed that her dog often engaged in scratching and agreed to come in the following morning.

Though she and Muffin arrived fifteen minutes late, all other patients were put on hold. While Kevin and Rodney searched the dog's raggedy coat, Rose, with hair as shaggy as her pet's, held her paw and cooed at her. Thirty-one fleas were found on Muffin, all a healthy reddish brown. Dr. Ahab recommended Kevin and Kit bathe her with a special shampoo to prevent further infestation and retreated to his office.

Rose took the news with composure, and while she sat in the waiting room and the doctor was defeatedly adding Muffin's information to his "Inspected" file, Rodney knocked on Dr. Ahab's door.

"Contact tracing," Rodney said, standing in his doorway. "Yes. We need to do more contact tracing. This time it might work, it might."

Dr. Ahab's dejected eye lit with hope. "Yes," he said, "as long as Rose didn't take Muffin to the dog park."

Later while Dr. Ahab, Rodney, Rose and Kevin gathered around the doctor's desk, Rodney explained to Rose the obligation they felt to assure the health of the local canine community.

"How can I help?" she said. She had little to do when it wasn't tax season.

"We're relying on you to tell us which dogs Muffin came into contact with since your last visit to Dr. English, we are."

Rose willingly revealed she lived on Dedham Street where she walked her dog three times a day.

"And do you take Muffin to the dog park, do you?"

"The dog park?" Rose looked troubled. "No, I don't. Muffin was once bit by a pit bull there. Dr. English had to stitch her up." Her eyes grew wistful with the memory of it. "We knew that pit bull for years, Petunia, a lovely dog, but she must have woken up on the wrong side of her crate that day. You never know what's going to happen in that dog park."

"And do you ever come into contact with other dogs on Dedham Street?" Rodney asked, with some relief.

Rose looked pensive, then finally said. "Only a German Shepherd that lives in the building. And once in a while Lady Augusta, from across the street."

"The board of health requires any information you have on these two dogs, they do," Rodney said.

Lyla, the German Shepherd belonged to Bill, an inventor of household gadgets, she told them, and as both worked at home, they saw each other outside the building walking their dogs at different times of the day.

Lady Augusta, an unshorn Shih Tzu, walked with her standoffish owner, Marina, early in the morning and after six in the evening, when Marina came home from work, Rose said. She didn't know her last name, but once elicited Marina's phone number when asking about a plumber she was using. "It took a lot for her to give me her number," Rose said. "I'm pretty sure we ran into her a few times last week. She'll let her precious dog sniff at Muffin every so often, but mostly tries to avoid us by crossing the street. Otherwise she puts up with us and grunts a few words if I try to talk to her. Our dogs seem to like each other, so they might have gotten close enough to exchange bugs, but I don't know for sure. I don't know her exact address, but her house is across the street from my building, so it must be 158 or 160 Dedham Street. A white split-level with a two-tiered birdbath on the front lawn."

"Have you run into any other dogs, have you?" Rodney asked, quickly writing down the information.

"We ran into a small, black mutt at the grocery store last week, maybe part toy poodle. They allow dogs inside. But I have no idea what the owner's name is. The dog's hair was dirty and matted, like she hadn't had a bath in months. And the same goes for her owner. She asked about Muffin, so I did most of the talking. If I had known I needed all this information—"

"But you couldn't have known, how could you?" Rodney said. "What's the name of the grocery store?"

Rose, an avid streamer of detective series, suddenly feeling like a witness of some heinous crime, began to dramatize the part. "Fred's Mart," she said. "It's on Manhattan Street. We were in the canned soups and vegetables aisle. She was a large woman in a flowery dress, short, grey hair and dangly earrings too stylish for the rest of her. I also noticed she was eating from a bag of M&Ms."

Rodney continued taking notes, omitting the soup aisle, the earrings and the M&Ms. After Rose gave them her neighbor's phone numbers and all left the office, Dr. Ahab went to Quiznos' desk and instructed her to phone both Bill and Marina and to lure them to the clinic as she had lured Rose.

"Tell them we're concerned about a neighborhood flea infestation, that the board of health recommends contact tracing, and you were referred by Rose Bouton. Tell them no charge, and we're willing to do a house call."

Quiznos, fully aware of the impetus for these demands, felt her opposition to Dr. Ahab's crusade reaching new heights. Initially contained within the walls of his clinic, the maniacal quest was now invading the town, imposing itself on its inhabitants, causing them upsets and inconveniences. Her loyalty to Dr. Ahab had so far prevented her from staging anything but small rebellious acts, and now was the time to conduct a more impactful protest, one she had lately been contemplating. For the time being she would continue her work in the clinic but affect a new persona. She would replace the real Quiznos with an android. She would look like Quiznos, dress like Quiznos, walk like Quiznos and perform all her receptionist's duties, but behave like a machine. Sympathy, empathy, compassion, warmth, kindness and understanding, all qualities necessary for dealing with emotional pet owners would be thrown by the wayside. She wouldn't make small talk, greet visitors by name, concern herself with treatments, offer coffee, tidy up the waiting room or bother with lost items. Most of all, she would make herself a stranger to Dr. Ahab. He was waiting for her response.

"Call them now?" she said, without lifting the end of her sentence.

"Now."

Dr. Ahab remained near her desk in rapid pacing listening to her speak into the receiver, envisioning his complete annihilation of the White Flea only days away. Her conversation was brief. Bill would bring Lyla to the clinic the following day at noon. She had been vomiting now and then for the past two weeks, and Bill had been meaning to have her examined anyway.

But her conversation with Marina was another matter. "Sorry dear," Dr. Ahab heard Quiznos say. "I didn't mean to insult you. . . I'm not accusing you . . .Yes, I'm sure you're very clean. . . I'm sure you love your dog very much. But the cleanliness of the dog has nothing to do with her ability to catch fleas . . . Yes, I believe your home is spotless . . . three times a week? It sounds very clean . . . No, before you hang up—we would do a very quick search, ten minutes at the most. You wouldn't have to bring your dog here. We could do a house call and be out of there in no time—"

"Tell her we can come right away," Dr. Ahab put in.

Quiznos couldn't help furrowing her brow at him. "What are you doing right now?" she continued. "We could—" Quiznos paused before replacing the receiver on the phone base. "She hung up," she said in her new monotone. "She says her dog is perfectly healthy, and she sees no reason to bother with our problem."

Dr. Ahab's hopes fell. He even thought of kidnapping the dog. But then his usually ponderous brain lit up. "If she lives in a house," he said, "there may be a yard where her dog may spend some time." He found Kevin and Rodney cleaning out the medication cabinet and gave them Marina's address. "Go to the house tomorrow morning around ten when the woman is at work. Bring your flea combs with you. Her dog should be in the yard."

Rodney dropped a bottle of expired pills into the trash bin. "What if she isn't?" he said. "Should we break in, should we?"

"Whatever it takes."

They did not have to break in. The next morning they found,

fenced inside the back yard, a chaise lounge, an outdoor dining set and the petite Lady Augusta lying in its shade, a pink clip gathering the hair on the top of her head and wrapped in long strands of brown and white hair. To Kevin she appeared to be buried under a rug. She rose as they approached and broke into a clamor of high-pitched barking, her tresses undulating with every woof.

The fence allowed them to insert the toes of their shoes into its gaps as they climbed it. Once safely inside the yard, Kevin said, "What's all that wheezing?"

"Shih Tzus have trouble breathing, they do," Rodney said over the noise. "She probably suffers from brachycephalic airway obstructive syndrome."

Kevin began to chase her, but the hard-breathing dog ran slowly and he easily overtook her, gathering up the mass of hair, almost surprised to feel a dog's body inside it. It was not easy to comb such a shaggy dog. Rodney tangled the hairs with his comb, twisting and tearing at them, then Kevin tried, almost blinded by the brightness of the sun and the whiteness of them. They shoved them this way and that, unsure of their progress, the dog breathing so loudly Kevin thought she might be in pain. But as they worked, she lay quietly enough, and he continued to remind himself the importance of searching this particular dog. She had made direct contact with Muffin, and Muffin with Moby.

It wasn't until the car motor shut off and a door slammed loudly that they feared someone had entered the house. They turned the dog on her back, and in a frenzy of smoothing and pulling on her hairs, both simultaneously combed her abdomen, the inside of her legs and her armpits, while shouting to each other:

.   "We already did that spot!"

"You're not going deep enough."

"You're throwing the hairs in my way!"

From within the house they heard the faint sound of a woman's voice calling, "Lady Augusta!"

"What do you think?" whispered Kevin.

"We're done." Rodney pocketed his comb and quickly rose.

The dog squirmed out of Kevin's grasp and emitted more chirpy barks while scurrying towards the back door. Kevin yelled, "Hide!" and he and Rodney ran to behind some small bushes at the far side of the yard, a laughable hiding place considering the low height of the plants and their paucity of leaves. Together they crouched, Kevin wishing he had not chosen to put on a fluorescent orange shirt that morning. He hissed at Rodney over the dog's barks. "This is insane. What are we doing? We could be arrested for trespassing. All for the sake of our crazy boss."

"Quiet," Rodney hissed back. "It'll be fine, it will."

The back door opened, and Marina appeared in pink and white selections of activewear. "Lady! Quiet!" She knelt before the barking dog. "You miss me? Oooooh, my little beauty. Who's the most beautiful dog in the world? You hungry? You want something to eat? C'mon." Kevin held his breath, sure that Marina would look up, but she only had eyes for her hirsute pet, and the two were soon inside the house. Kevin and Rodney escaped the yard in a furor of darting and fence climbing, clumsily but without a scratch, then raced down Dedham Street.

At the same time, Bill was arriving at Dr. Ahab's clinic with the rambunctious and irritated Lyla. The doctor tried his best to keep the German Shepherd calm while conducting a long and thorough search on her, leaving no hair unturned and no fold of skin unchecked, but found not one flea on her. He seldom conducted searches alone, but when he did, the length of time spent on each was increasing. Lately, contemplating his thoroughness, he was unable to stop himself from wondering if had missed a spot under a collar or inside a back leg. Just one more area to look at, he would think, rarely changing the outcome of a search.

The morning had proven unproductive, both Lyla and Lady Augusta clean of fleas. But Dr. Ahab would not be discouraged. Later that afternoon he sent Kevin and Rodney to the dog park to pursue the one remaining dog on Rose's list, the black mutt resembling a toy poodle, and if they had no luck there, they should look for it at Fred's Mart. They found no trace of such a dog in either location, and the doctor had no choice but to add it to his long list of elusive suspects.

XVIII

OBJECTIONS

Whenever Gabriel appeared in the clinic, Kevin made a point of conducting all flea searches behind the locked door of the X-ray room and drowned all fleas he discovered in his bowl of soapy water. There was a loose screw inside Gabriel's head, he decided, and the more time he spent with him, the more that screw seemed to turn in the wrong direction.

After a two-week absence, the doctor's son reappeared one day wearing a red beret angled low on his forehead, a pair of heavy military boots and a large yellow pin with the black letters ILF fixed to his T-shirt. Rodney assigned Kevin and Gabriel to bathe Tammy, an Old English Sheepdog with a matted coat and smelling of yeast, and while Gabriel held the dog and Kevin sprayed her grey, fuzzy strands with water, he asked Gabriel what the initials on his pin stood for.

Gabriel seemed to live under the illusion that whatever he knew was common knowledge. "The Insect Liberation Front, of course," he said, with an air of irritation.

"And what does the Insect Liberation Front do?"

Gabriel paused, collected his patience and answered. "We believe in the protection of all insects."

Kevin questioned the existence of such a group, and though the button appeared authentic, wondered if Gabriel was its sole member, and if this was a direct attack on his father's quest. While the two of them scrubbed the dog with a medicated shampoo, Gabriel subjected him to an increasingly passionate lecture.

"Every day millions of insects die because of human carelessness. People step on them, they crush them willy nilly. These people are murderers just like any other murderer, killers of innocent beings that never harmed anyone. Farmers make a profit from the misery and death of insects. No one out there defends these animals. The problem is prejudice. People think insects are ugly. They judge them by their looks, not their souls. Insects are just regular beings trying to survive like everyone else. They're not evil. They can't help it if they need animal blood to survive.

"The ILF believes in protecting the lives of insects. We place them back into nature where they can live out their natural lives, free from suffering. We expose cruel experiments performed on insects in laboratories. We are an international organization that cannot be smashed, cannot be infiltrated and cannot be stopped. Because insects are unable to fight back themselves, we have the moral right to engage in reciprocal acts. Already two such acts have been committed against offenders in Sweden and the Philippines. This clinic, with its policy of killing fleas, is an enemy of the ILF. If a member of the ILF witnesses an act offending the cause of insect liberation, steps will be taken!"

Kevin helped Gabriel towel the sheepdog dry with shaky hands. After Gabriel left the room and, as the dog required a haircut, he called Rodney in and, as quietly and calmly as possible, repeated to him the essence of the diatribe just delivered to him.

Rodney's eyes grew wide. "Reciprocal acts, what? What

would those acts be?"

Rodney alerted Kit and Quiznos, and five minutes later, while Gabriel sat at the employee room iMac on happyveggies.com, the group knocked on Dr. Ahab's office door. They found him inside studying a print-out of a map of Nanford, each apartment or house where a dog resided marked with a red X. Their interruption annoyed him, but after hearing their report, he focused on them with a concerned eye.

"Your son is threatening this clinic with acts of terrorism," Quiznos told him. "We're afraid for our lives."

Dr. Ahab had long been dealing with Gabriel's rebellious behavior and would have preferred to ignore it. His son's threats of violence were no doubt empty, but he needed to preserve the allegiance and well-being of his workers. "Acts of terrorism you say?" He pressed on his intercom lever and spoke into the box. "Gabriel, please come to my office." Then he sat back in his chair and shook his head. His optimistic expression, sparked by the recent bout of contact tracing, had completely vanished.

"After his mother died, I was a neglectful parent. This impudent behavior is the result of my indifference to him and my preoccupation with my work. I take full responsibility for it. I forced him to compete for my attention with every four legged creature that enters this clinic. It's no wonder he dresses like Che Guevara. I must repair the damage I've done, but at this moment, more pressing matters occupy my mind."

The four nervous workers left, but found it difficult to resume their duties over the ruckus issuing from Dr. Ahab's office, Gabriel's angry voice and the banging and shoving of furniture. Finally the office door swung open, and Gabriel hustled to the clinic door, shouting, "Damn you! I'll find another vet to work for, one who appreciates me!"

After two weeks, with no sign of Gabriel, all breathed easier.

XIX

FLEAS IN CULTURE

A mysterious looking painting hung in the entryway of Dr. Ahab's office building, one that Kevin never found time to linger before. It was a sodden, dingy picture, enough to drive him to distraction, but held an indefinite sublimity that froze him to it. At last he decided that only by diligent study, repeated visits to it and by asking others' opinions would he be able to fully grasp its meaning.

One morning, woken by the grating sound of a nearby cement mixer, he arrived early enough to work to be able to stop and examine the painting. In the uneven light of the entryway window, he peered at its smoky and defaced surface that by its shades and shadows made him wonder if it was the result of the attempt of some ambitious young artist to portray chaos bewitched. But most confounding was a squirmy, multi-legged form dead center, floating in a cloudy yeast. Was it a mass of life breaking up the stream of time, or did it bear a faint resemblance to a gigantic bug? In fact, yes, the picture represented an insect, maybe a flea, and had probably been hung there in connection with Dr. Ahab's clinic.

Kevin spent much of the day haunted by the image, by the large scale of the tiny bug and the darkness it lay in, and tried to wipe it out of his mind by viewing more pleasant and comprehensible images, by googling impressionist paintings and past winners of the Westminster Dog Show. But even as he walked home then dined with Weewag, he thought of the painting, even as they played tug of war and a quick game of fetch.

He had to assume Charity was as well-versed in the arts as she was in all the other topics they had discussed over the weeks, and he accepted her proposal they see each other the next evening with more eagerness than usual.

The oppressive July heat and the breezeless air slowed their pace as they made their way down Wapping Street to the dog park, either leading or pulled by Stella and Weewag and sipping freezer-cold, fruit-flavored sparkling waters.

Kevin waited with patience until Charity finished describing the new self-checkout machines installed in the library that, instead of easing her job, seemed to be complicating it. After expressing the appropriate amount of sympathy, he was finally able to ask, "What do you know about fleas in art? Do they commonly appear, and what do they represent?"

Charity answered without hesitation, not to Kevin's surprise. "Artists have always found the flea a very curious creature. We talk freely about sex now, but historically it has been a taboo subject, especially in the Victorian era, when the flea became the preferred metaphor for sex."

Kevin was sorry he had brought up the subject but didn't see how he could have predicted the connection between a tiny, ugly insect and an intimate act between two people. No two topics could have had less in common. The word 'sex' coming from Charity's lips and uttered in her sweet tones troubled Kevin, as he was not yet sure where to place her in his life.

"Do you know John Donne's poem, 'The Flea'?" she said.

They had reached their usual bench in the dog park, and as soon as they sat, Charity began to recite:

> Mark but this flea, and mark in this,
> How little that which thou deniest me is;
> It sucked me first, and now sucks thee,
> And in this flea our two bloods mingled be;
> Thou know'st that this cannot be said
> A sin, nor shame, nor loss of maidenhead,
> Yet this enjoys before it woo,
> And pampered swells with one blood made of two,
> And this, alas, is more than we would do.

"I'm not familiar with that poem," Kevin said, having recoiled at every innuendo, wondering what kind of man John Donne was and hoping he kept his poems short.

"And have you ever read *The Autobiography of a Flea*?" Charity went on. "It's narrated by a flea who describes sex between nuns and priests. The flea can move from body to body, so he has a good view of the action."

"No, I haven't." His brain spun with the effort of finding a new topic of discussion.

"It was written in eighteen eighty-seven, can you believe it? And fleas appear in paintings, too. In the eighteenth-century, fleas were a common problem for everyone in all classes and would live in beds, inside wigs, on pets, you name it. The French word for flea is *puce* which is where the color puce comes from. It's a purplish brown, like a brown flea squashed with red blood. There are quite a few paintings that show beautiful women looking for fleas on their bodies. The implications are they are pregnant out of wedlock or prostitutes."

So taken with Charity's words, Kevin barely noticed only a few feet before him a small, black mutt with curly, matted hair chasing a ball. It was taller and skinnier than a toy poodle but, with its dangling ears and furry snout, did resemble one. A large woman in a loose dress with a flowery print had thrown the ball. Charity took his gasp for a reaction to her information. "Yes," she said, "it's true. The flea is not looked at in an admirable light, not in the arts."

Kevin tried to refocus on Charity. "Puce?" He looked back at the small, black dog, now heading to the gate with its owner. "I have to go," he blurted, then called to Weewag.

"Oh," Charity said. "So suddenly?"

"Yes, it's a work thing." He shouted again to his dog as he headed towards him, and Charity stood as Kevin attached his dog's leash to his collar.

"I'll go with you," she called. "Where are you going?"

"You wouldn't enjoy it." He and Weewag hurried towards the gate. "I'll call you," he shouted back to her.

Charity wore a puzzled look but gave him a compliant wave and watched as they quickly exited the park. Anyway, Stella was immersed in a small group of dogs tumbling and climbing over each other, and she and Charity would have been slow to catch up with them.

Kevin found it difficult to follow the little black dog and its owner without being seen, as the owner appeared to be patient and easygoing, and rather than her walking her dog, it seemed the dog was walking her. Kevin and Weewag followed them to a neighborhood of houses in staggering disrepair with dirty and dented cars parked in front of them. He saw sagging foundations, boarded-up windows and dried up lawns. As most of the tree trunks that stood between him and his prey were too scrawny to hide behind, twice he was forced to lead Weewag to behind a parked car and then some sparsely leafed corner bushes.

The coat of the black mutt looked dirty enough to be hosting any number of fleas. At one point, while the dog released a healthy pile of excrement and as Kevin hid with Weewag behind a parked delivery truck, he had time to mull over Charity's words about the flea in art, tried to imagine a painting depicting a flea running over a beautiful woman's bare limbs and resisted the urge to then and there take out his phone to find such an image. Then he pictured John Donne at his writing desk and wondered why he had chosen the flea as a metaphor for sex over other ectoparasites like tapeworms, ticks or head lice. Maybe it was its noseless face, bad posture or silly hanging appendages. Yes, in his attack on Dr. Ahab, Moby had acted on instinct and could be considered guiltless, but he remained a flea, an insect whose once-innocent character was now debased and dishonorable.

So deep in reverie, Kevin lost watch on his marks and suddenly realized they had disappeared. He assumed they had turned the next corner but, upon reaching it, saw no trace of them and scolded himself for allowing thoughts of the tiny bug to distract him. It did not deserve such contemplation.

On the driveway of the nearest corner house, a small red item, maybe a button, drew his attention, and he soon identified it as an M&M. Remembering Rose mentioning that the woman in the grocery store had been eating M&Ms, he thought, this could well be the home of that very woman. And the house, by its rotting appearance and decaying steps reinforced with small planks of wood haphazardly nailed together, could have very well been the home of a flea-ridden dog. The name on the mailbox read "Mapple."

XX

ANOTHER ATTACK

Kevin's photos of both the house and the dog in all their decrepit splendor sparked Dr. Ahab's imagination. Once more he summoned Kit, who easily succeeded in identifying the owner and her dog as Martha Mapple and Athena. Though he was unable to discover her phone number or email address on her Facebook page, he sent her a friend request that she immediately accepted and, with the doctor's approval, and, after writing a private message to his newly found ex, he sent Martha a private message announcing to her a flea epidemic of some proportion and offering Athena a free check-up by Dr. Ahab if she called his number. The doctor apprised Quiznos of the possibility of the call and the urgency to see Athena, and Quiznos gave him a mechanical nod of acknowledgement.

The call came late the next morning. Martha told Quiznos she rarely checked her Facebook messages but, through a haphazard series of clicks, Kit's note suddenly appeared. Quiznos showed no interest in the happenstance and repeated to Martha in her practiced flat tones Dr. Ahab's request she come in as soon as possible. Martha promised to arrive with Athena that afternoon, and Quiznos rescheduled Mrs. Heidenhammer and her Pekingese, MacBeth, telling her a terrorist threat in the building had caused an evacuation. When Mrs. Heidenhammer expressed vexation over this inconvenience, Quiznos remained stony.

Martha's phone call threw the doctor and crew into a frenzy of preparation, all cans and spray bottles readied. No sooner did she and Athena arrive than Rodney led them to the examination room and easily lifted the small dog onto the silver table. While Athena stood patiently, he found no fleas on her, but when he turned her onto her back, and while Kevin and the doctor stood by, an unexpected visitor arrived, Gabriel, having added a military jacket and camouflage pants to his already threatening ensemble.

"Another flea search?" His eyes lit with fire.

But Dr. Ahab was intent on the search, imagining the dog a piñata full of fleas, one of them Moby. "Yes, Gabriel. Would you mind backing away?" he said. "Kevin, take the Demon Killer."

Gabriel quickly approached then held his hand a few inches over the dog's stomach. "I forbid it!"

"Please remove your hand, Gabriel," Dr. Ahab said with all the patience he could muster. He held his bottle high.

"You know what you search for?"

"Yes, I'm searching for fleas, like any good doctor would."

"Is it the White Flea? The one that took your eye? is it Moby the flea? I tried to get Dr. Goney to hire me. I thought he might appreciate a hard-working young man like me who has real compassion for all animals, but no vet around here will hire a son of yours! They call you a crazy old man, sick with vengeance against an animal the size of a cookie crumb! This search has to stop! That flea has the right to live out his days in peace! A murderous action will reap murderous results. I have people to report to!"

Though inside the doctor, a flame headed towards a stick of dynamite, an unwillingness to stir up deeper passions in his already enraged son stole over him, and he managed to maintain his cool. "It's nothing but a flea search, Gabriel. Please leave us to it."

To Kevin's utter amazement, peering over Gabriel's hand, he was able to spot, running across the dog's chest, a flea of the palest color. He couldn't help but shout, "But—it's the White Flea! It's Moby!"

In spite of the insect's history of violence, all stooped to peer closely at it. Indeed, though its pace was quick, it appeared like flashing white neon.

"Let me be the one to kill it, let me!" Rodney cried.

"You may not!" Gabriel's hand remained an obstacle to all as they peered around it trying to follow the path of the flea as it headed towards him, reaching the fur on the dog's right side.

Kevin's spirits sank. Once again he had been mistaken. The reflection of the overhead lights on the flea's back made it look white, especially in contrast to the dark fur around it. Dr. Ahab, too, saw the flea was brown and not his true enemy, but he was ready to defy his son. He spoke in a hoarse whisper. "Stay calm, stay calm! Rodney, take the Pestracide. Hold your spray cans ready! Keep your voices down!"

As they obeyed, Gabriel maintained his defiant stance, and with his other hand, drew his phone from his pocket and set it to camera. "There will be evidence!"

The flea was not Moby but possibly a close relative. Like a tiny missile, it hurled itself from the dog's side directly at Gabriel's left ear. Gabriel dropped his phone and held his lobe with both hands. "Owwww," he cried, his eyes shut tight with pain. "Owww, my ear!" Kevin and the doctor tried to pry his hands from the side of his head to kill the assailant supposedly trapped there, and Gabriel finally allowed them to inspect. But no flea swam through the stream of blood flowing from his earlobe.

While Gabriel applied an antiseptic, Kevin and Rodney completed a thorough search of the dog's underside finding fifteen fleas, none of them white. Gabriel wrapped his ear in gauze then took the two aspirin his father prescribed. After scolding all for scaring the poor, helpless insect into a blind attack, one it was forced to wage out of sheer instinct and self-defense, he turned down the duties Rodney assigned him and left the clinic muttering how he was now scarred for life.

XXI

A STRONG INSECTICIDE

Not having seen Gabriel for nearly a month, with the confidence he would not return, Dr. Ahab removed the spray bottles and cans of insecticide from their hiding place in the examination room cabinet and placed them on the counter. He assigned Kit the task of periodically holding them upside down and giving each a squirt to keep the nozzles clean.

One day as they sat gleaming by a sunlit window like an improbable still life, Dr. Ahab stood studying them with a skeptical eye. Yes, these were more effective than Gabriel's eco-friendly brands which now lay at the bottom of the trash bin, but only incrementally. Their promises to exterminate pests seemed empty, the words on their labels only advertising ploys. Kevin watched the doctor unscrew the trigger on one of the plastic bottles, pour its contents down the sink then raise it high.

"The spray is not yet invented that will kill Moby the Flea," he said. "Here in this hand I will hold his death! I will cook up a spray ten times as strong as the others to attack the most vulnerable part of the flea, where the flea most feels his damned life!" And he promptly phoned an old college acquaintance, Weston Perth, a chemist. Long ago, Weston had declared himself always available to concoct a pesticide that would leave no flea alive. Sincere and obliging, he held his test tubes with a patient hand.

He arrived at Dr. Ahab's clinic the next day promptly at four o'clock. The light from Dr. Ahab's office window played on his eager eye as Weston sat across from him.

"What are the choices?" the doctor said.

Weston, about sixty years old and slightly hunched, had forgotten to remove his safety glasses. "You have your IGRs—insect growth inhibitors—and your insecticides," he said, appearing unnecessarily shielded.

"And which work the best?"

"The IGRs kill by interrupting the life cycle. They mimic hormones in young insects preventing maturity, thereby stopping them from reproducing. Some arrest the proper formation of the exoskeleton, others will disrupt the development of the larvae, killing the pupa and causing the eggs to be sterile."

"I have no time for life cycles. What about the insecticides?"

"You have your Etofenprox—"

"And what does that do?"

"It's a pyrethroid derivative that—"

"Pyro—what?"

"Pyrethroid derivatives are similar to pyrethrins drawn from the chrysanthemum flower." Though aware of the doctor's glazed look, Weston continued. He loved his work and had few people to discuss it with. "Etofenprox opens the sodium ion channels in the nerve cells of the insect causing them to fire spontaneously. The insect will go into spasms and die."

"Spasms? Good. Are these spasms painful?"

The chemist hesitated. "I can't say, Doctor."

"What are my other choices?"

Weston looked askance. "Fipronil."

"And what does Fipronil do?"

"It blocks the production and action of cholinesterase, an

essential nervous system enzyme, paralyzing the insect and causing it to keel over and die."

"Paralysis. That sounds good too. Spasms or paralysis. Can we do both?"

The chemist himself looked slightly paralyzed. "I'm sure we can, Doctor. And you might want to add a little piperonyl butoxide."

"How fast does that kill?"

"It doesn't. But it enhances the potency of pyrethroids. It's a semisynthetic derivative of safrole, found in sassafras plants."

"Natural, huh? Yes, it's good to be natural. But we don't want to be too natural. And do these blend well together?"

"I think so, Doctor."

"What percentage of Etofenprox?"

"I recommend point five percent."

"Point five? Not much, is it? Can we make it point six?"

"I'm afraid not. Not if we care about the dogs."

Dr. Ahab's one eye, now capable of as much expression as two, stared at the chemist in deep contemplation. "All right," he finally said. "We don't want to hurt the dogs, do we?" After a few seconds' thought, he said, "We'll call it Perthacide."

XXII

A PROTEST

One early August evening the temperature remained so high that even the most rambunctious dogs in the park lounged under a bench or in the meager shade of its single tree. Kevin enviously watched a collie enjoying the spray of the available hose as her owner tried to cool her down. He sat with Charity in a comfortable silence, while nearby a particular grey puppy with lifted ears angled his head at his owner as if trying to understand his words.

"Dogs must be frustrated creatures," Kevin said. "Sometimes Weewag looks like he really wants to know what I'm saying."

"Nonsense," Charity said. "You mean the head tilt? That means Weewag is assessing the situation. He's using his ears to gauge the level and tone of your voice to read your emotions. And dogs like to be spoken to. They think it will lead to some kind of reward. Dogs will spend more time with you if you talk to them. I hate to say it, but they love baby talk."

"I would never speak baby talk to Weewag. I respect him too much." Kevin lifted his hand to shield his face from the setting sun. "And what about all that fur they have to wear in this weather? It seems one of nature's biggest mistakes."

"Actually, their coats insulate their bodies against the heat," Charity said, "and keep them cool." But she was tired of the subject of dogs. After the appropriate amount of seconds passed, she said, "By the way, I've been meaning to ask you. What do you do at your job? I mean, did you study to become a vet?" As if to give the impression his answer would not be of great importance, she picked up a ball that had rolled over to them and, with a powerful arm, sent it hurling.

But Kevin had been waiting for such a question, one that meant she was assessing his qualifications for long term companionship. Despite his low status in the clinic, he was glad to give her an honest answer and leave her to judge its importance. But he would not be too truthful. The distraction Charity provided continued to be pleasurable, and Kevin had long ago chosen not to destroy it by mentioning Dr. Ahab's mania. What would be the consequence? She might listen in horror then advise him to quit his job. Or maybe she would insist he report Dr. Ahab to the AVMA. Worse, she might find the doctor an object of sympathy and encourage Kevin to continue helping him. Even worse, she might volunteer to join the quest herself.

"No, I'm an assistant," he said. "I do a variety of things, not very interesting."

"Come on. You can tell me at least something," Charity said.

"I do flea searches."

"Yes, I know. You bring up fleas quite a lot, actually. Is there a particular reason, or is it just because you work for a veterinarian?"

"No reason. But after you told me about the part they play in art and literature, I don't feel so bad about killing them. I had no idea they were so disreputable."

"And I haven't told you the worst of it." She adopted a dramatic tone. "Did you know they were a vector in all the bubonic plagues that have terrorized the world, and are responsible for the deaths of millions of people?"

Kevin squinted at her. "I thought the plagues were caused by rats."

"Rats infected with the bacteria that causes the plague were bitten by fleas, then the fleas bit humans, transferring the bacteria to them."

Charity suggested they get up and walk in order to cure her restlessness after sitting in the library all day. She stood, called to Stella, and they began to head to the gate but, stunned by her words, Kevin remained seated.

"Wait a minute, Charity," he called but, out of her earshot, he had no choice but to gather Weewag then catch up with her and Stella as they exited the park. As the four of them strolled Palmetto Street, Kevin said, "I had no idea fleas caused the world so much misery."

"But I haven't told you the worst of it."

"How much lower can the flea go?"

"Recently in China they found fossils of giant fleas from the age of the dinosaurs, about ten times larger than today's fleas. They showed a wingless insect remarkably similar to the flea down to the mouthparts. Entomologists have always wondered why the flea's stinger seems built for a much tougher skin than a dog's. They found traces of bacteria on the mouthparts of these fossils similar to the bacteria that caused the bubonic plagues. So it's highly possible the dinosaur fleas transferred some kind of plague to the dinosaurs, wiping them out."

Kevin felt rattled. The idea of the flea as a greater murderer than Hitler, Stalin and Mao put together made him light-headed. Astonishment replaced even his most remote romantic notions involving Charity. He wanted to immediately go home and consult Wikipedia. He finally interrupted her as she was expounding on the health problems of the Stegosaurus.

"About the cause of the extinction of the dinosaurs—"

She gave him a curious look. "Yes?"

"I mean—how many scientists think it might be the flea?"

But Weewag's barking was his only answer, directed at a wind-up toy in the form of a small plastic bird speeding down the sidewalk, chased by a laughing child. The dog was causing enough commotion that after Kevin calmed him, it seemed Charity had forgotten his question. She continued on the topic of the dinosaur diet which let to a discussion of which foods each of them preferred. Forty-five minutes later he hardly realized they had arrived at her front walk.

Earlier that afternoon, anticipating seeing her, Kevin wondered if she were expecting the evening to end with more than just "see you!" After all, they had known each other for more than a month, and Charity was making it increasingly obvious she wanted more contact between them than infrequent hand-holding. When considering her character, her firm step and the tightness of her skirts, shyness did not come to mind, but it seemed she was patiently waiting for some manifestation of his feelings. This proved difficult as not only was he unsure of his own but of Weewag's as well. Kevin and Charity were never without their dogs, so there was no choice but to kiss in front of them. That afternoon he had considered proposing they leave them home, but never remembered to do so.

This new problem dimmed Kevin's thoughts of the disgrace of the flea. They hung in the air to be pondered later. But they had caused him more blindness towards Charity than usual. He lost sight of her hair as it glistened in the glare of her exterior door light, of her eyes that shone bright even behind the thick lenses of her glasses. She had simply become the bearer of bad news. I have to step up, Kevin thought. This is a seminal moment that calls for my complete attention. We have been working towards this moment for some time now, and I can't destroy it.

They stood in front of her house in the cooling air, listening to the hum of the neighborhood air-conditioners. "Well," she said. She removed her glasses and tilted her chin slightly towards him as a light breeze blew her hair off her face. "It was a lovely time." She drew near to him.

He stammered that it was indeed. Stella was watching them out of the corner of her eye, and Weewag was sniffing the sidewalk, tugging slightly on his leash, as if ready to head home.

Kevin drew his face near Charity's. But their lips barely touched when a cacophony of barking erupted, echoing throughout the street. The ear-splitting noise contained a small percentage of anger but mostly jealousy and the need for attention. Both dogs leapt at them as if to prevent them not from kissing, but from killing each other.

Both Kevin and Charity demanded their dogs to quiet, Kevin pretending to be angrier than he felt. As soon as they separated, Charity smoothed her hair, bent down and leaned towards Weewag. "Weewag," she sang, "Do you want a kiss too?" She kissed the top of the dog's head, then the head of her own dog.

As Kevin led Weewag home, his mind whirled with confusion. Charity's admirable qualities, those he rarely found in anyone, should have been melting his heart, as it seemed he had melted hers. He was well aware of her pretty face, shiny hair and the way she filled her tank top, but he only wanted to look at her the same way one looks at a beautifully carved statue. He had no idea why she didn't succeed in wakening his deepest feelings, why he rarely thought about her, dreamed about her or had a strong desire to cook her dinner.

He wondered if Weewag was the reason, if it were possible for a dog to substitute for a life mate, an animal with the intelligence of a two-year-old child, who offered no challenges and completely depended on him. Was there something specifically about Charity that did not agree with him, or was Kevin developing an indifference to all women, and would this indifference prevent him from leading a normal life? But how to define normal, and what did it matter? Then again, God's idea of a mate for Adam was a woman, not a dog.

Yes, his dog possessed endless qualities to revel in, but Kevin had to admit it, that all dogs were far more barbaric, simple and motley creatures than humans. All that week every time he looked at Weewag, the vague disquietude he had begun to feel increased, heightened at times by the dog's uncalled for and incoherent barking at loud machines or honking car horns.

These thoughts having concluded—whether or not to his satisfaction—his brain was now free to address what had formerly preoccupied him, Charity's words about the malevolent flea. Did an animal that caused so much misery in the world have the right to exist and for what reason? Murderous people were condemned and executed, and the flea was in close competition with the worst of them. One evening sitting at his laptop, Kevin soon found that though the flea was a food source for frogs, snakes, ants, lizards, beetles and spiders, each predator had an extensive list of alternate food options. Without the flea, no one's survival would be compromised.

One entomologist claimed fleas helped dead things rot and enriched the soil, very useful to someone, he supposed. He found more vague sentences about the flea helping to research human diseases, disorders and their cures but with no specifics. All seemed like desperate attempts to justify the existence of an insect who lived only to irritate.

Maybe his own prejudice was at fault, and his attitude needed to be changed. After all, flea circuses had entertained millions and had earned their operators wealth and fame and, over the years, the sinister character of the flea inspired a great many artists and writers in need of the perfect metaphor. But considering the angst he daily witnessed, he could not help thinking that if the flea had never existed, it would not have been missed by anyone.

XXIII

WORK INSANITY

Quiznos too was questioning her own reason for existence, mainly in connection with her work in the clinic. Maybe an automated phone system should have been installed and a website set up where patients could schedule their own appointments. Her new personality as an automaton now perfected—even her walk had become stiff and her movements jerky—was attracting no notice. She might as well have put on a British accent and pretended to be the queen. So invisible, she rarely received a please or thank you or an inquiry into her health. Even her new pair of Fontainebleau earrings earned her no compliments.

But one morning when the waiting room had cleared and she was tidying her files, Dr. Ahab stopped at her desk.

"I had a dream last night," he said. "I dreamt about two hearses."

At this demand for a human response, Quiznos froze. She could pretend not to understand him, but she held a strong belief in the existence of other worlds and dimensions, and her role as the clinic spiritual guide—one no robot ever performed with any degree of success—earned her so much joy and satisfaction, she was unable to fight the urge to counsel anyone in need. Over the years she had predicted the survival of many of Dr. Ahab's waning pets and the unfortunate deaths of a few.

She had guided him through the birth of his son and helped him mourn his dead wife.

She had no choice but to answer him, the warmth and sincerity of her voice restored (at which he showed no surprise). "I told you, Doctor," she said, "you dreamt that before. Those hearses can't be yours. What sizes were they?"

"They were meant for dogs, but—"

"You see? You were dreaming of your dead patients."

"I was, was I? There might be some truth to that. What do your cards say? The last time you read them, you told me I would kill the White Flea and live to tell the tale. Or will the flea kill me?"

Quiznos cleared her desk, produced her deck of tarot cards and arranged six in the pentagram spread. The doctor watched as she studied the colorful pictures before her. "Here's another prediction, Doctor," Quiznos said, her eyes flashing like the high beams of a car. "You will not be killed by the flea. You will be killed by a rope."

"A rope?"

"Yes, a rope."

"You mean a noose?"

"I can't get more specific than that."

He pondered for a moment. "Never! If I kill anyone, it won't be myself, it will be that flea. It's the pursuit of that flea that keeps me alive." Dr. Ahab's dark laughter sent a chill running through her. "I will not die by a rope or any other means. I am immortal then. Immortal!"

He headed back to his office leaving Quiznos staring after him. With unsettled nerves she tidied up her desk then sat very still, unable to resume her work. Soon she rose and headed to the doctor's office door. Even as her heart fluttered, she had no choice but to knock on it. When he called, "Come in," she took a deep breath and stepped inside.

She spoke to his right ear and the grey locks of hair around it as he peered at his computer screen. "Doctor Ahab," she said, "a better woman than me might let you off on something I'd resent in a younger and happier man."

With each of her words, the steel beam of his mind grew stronger. He turned towards her. "Damn it, Quiznos, are you critical of me? Out of my office!"

"No, Doctor, not yet. I beg you. I'm trying to be patient. Shouldn't we try to understand each other? You are not immortal. You're the same as everyone else in this clinic. We're all flesh and blood. One day we will all meet our maker."

Dr. Ahab's one eye spun. "There is one god that rules this earth and one doctor who rules this clinic. Out, Quiznos!"

Heat rushing to her face, as calmly as possible she turned away from him, paused for an instant, turned back and said, "You make me angry, Doctor, but you haven't insulted me. But don't beware of me, beware of yourself. Beware of yourself, Doctor."

"You pretend to be brave," Dr. Ahab said almost to himself, "but nevertheless you obey me. Please leave me to my lunch."

Dr. Ahab reached for the brown paper bag that lay on his desk. She backed out of the office, shut the door with a quiet click then stood outside it for a few seconds waiting for her heartbeats to subside. Then she went to the examination room where she found Rodney speaking on the phone, Kevin sweeping and Kit constructing a small sculpture with tongue depressors that, upon hearing her footsteps, he immediately crushed.

In as calm a tone as possible, she called to them. "Kevin, Kit, I need to talk to you. Rodney? This is important." She waited in the X-ray room until all were present, then closed the door tightly. She faced them and spoke with an earnest intonation. "The man we work for is insane." She knew she had stated the obvious, but hearing it aloud in her own voice increased its gravity and certainty. "He thinks he's immortal," Quiznos went on, "like a god! He has complete control of everyone in this miserable place. He's a horrid old man who says there's no one above him. He makes us all crazy, but we have no choice but to help him. I'm tied to him with no knife to cut the rope. I do what he says, and I hate him at the same time, and then I feel sorry for him. We all blindly follow him as he chases after that damned flea that's probably long dead by now. If we don't watch out, we'll all end up just as crazy as he is. We have to fight this insanity!"

"How can we?" Kevin said. "What can we do? Get him therapy? Antidepressants? Have him committed? There's no way out but to quit."

"Yes, quit!" Quiznos was delighted to hear her solution affirmed. "We should quit this job now before we're all stricken with the disease! We can't give into it! There's nothing we can do but walk out this door and never come back. We have to work together, all of us."

Kevin knew that Quiznos spoke the truth, but her words came too late. Inside all three young men an irrepressible fire had long been burning. Personal wants and needs had given way to one common goal, and there was no going back. Kevin felt the doctor's pain as if it were his own. He often closed one eye to experience navigating the world half blind and felt alarm at the flatness of his vision. His employer did not deserve this misfortune, and the fear he spread among his workers was wholly unintended. They gave into it because they recognized the same fallibility in themselves—that they, too, could fall victim to their own mad emotions.

"No, Quiznos," Kevin said. "We have to stick by him. We can't abandon him now, when he needs us most. Leaving him alone will only make him worse."

The rigor of Kevin's words took Quiznos by surprise. Of the three workers, he had struck her as the most levelheaded. She waited for him to back down, but when he spoke no further, she turned to Rodney. "Rodney what about you? For fourteen years you've stood by the doctor's side. You've seen what he's become. Don't you want to help him? Or has he taken over your mind too?"

Rodney angled his head to one side, considering. "I never know whether to shake him by the shoulders or pray for him, I don't. Yes, it's a strange thought, but he's strange too. He's about the strangest old man I ever worked for, he is. Is he mad? I don't know. There's definitely something on his mind, there is. He sleeps badly, he tells me. I guess his conscience keeps him awake.

"And I have been acting against my principles. I have. But it wasn't his fault I tried to cause a flea infestation in the park. I did it on my own. No one told me to. He does order more than a few flea searches, he does. But is that so terrible? It may be strange, but this is a veterinary clinic, it is. Maybe it's odd that an old man is chasing a particular flea, yes, but Dr. Ahab is our boss and it's not our place to question him, it's not. I say we should be patient. He has a genuine concern for animals. You should have seen him when my Natasha passed. He wept over the dog as if she was his own, he did. This'll blow over soon. No one can chase a flea forever. No one."

Quiznos, shaken by both Rodney and Kevin's words, could not imagine the extent of their vulnerability. Only exorcism could free them from such allegiance. She turned to Kit thinking surely his sharp mind would see the sense in her solution.

"Kit?" Quiznos said. "You see the doctor with clear eyes, don't you? You recognize madness when you see it. I'm going to walk out of this clinic and never come back. Will you join me? When the doctor realizes what he's lost, he may even call us back."

Kit stared at her dumbly, then shook his head. "Yeah, sometimes he's a little weird, but so are a lot of people. Most times he seems perfectly normal. I mean, he treats the dogs good, and he treats me good too. He's good at his job, and he's good to the dog owners. He never gets mad at me when I screw up, and he even offered to get me therapy for my phobia and pay for it too. I can't quit my job now. Mostly, I need money for school."

Quiznos felt the disappointment of her defeat. She had spent much of her life as a medical receptionist, quietly dealing with patients and their schedules, and   staging a mutiny was not her strong suit. One on one she might lecture the dog owners and sway their opinions, but groups were another matter. But the support of her co-workers wasn't imperative. She was an independent woman who for most of her life lived alone, and she was prepared and willing to act on her own. As she turned to leave, they called to her to come back and reconsider, but she would not.

She returned to her desk, sat at her computer and scoured the AVMA website until she read, "Reporting Concerns or Complaints. Contact your state veterinary medical association." On her state website she found, "File a complaint against a licensed professional," then dialed the number.

She reached an automated voice asking her to hold, then was subjected to a recording of a once cheerful but now corroded, skipping tape of possibly a waltz by Johann Strauss. After fifteen minutes she hung up, mostly to relieve her ears of the noise. She noticed it was twelve-thirty, that the waiting room was filling up with the afternoon patients, and the doctor's lunch hour was over. She buzzed him and when he answered, asked in her mechanical tone if he were ready for his next patient. When he answered in the affirmative, she dutifully called to the owner of a white-haired Pointer with a cast on his right front leg. "The doctor will see you now."

By the time the Pointer and his owner arrived, Dr. Ahab was in the examination room reading the dog's chart. Kevin, seeing the dog, reminded the doctor that a week before he had found it free of fleas and suggested he might take his lunch hour now. He was eager to walk with Weewag on Palmetto Street where they might meet up with a friendly Irish Setter they'd recently met, owned by an amiable matronly woman. After the doctor gave his consent, Kevin headed to the clinic door quickly passing Quiznos' desk. He came to a stop. She wasn't there. Had she had truly walked out on her job? She might be in the ladies room or in the kitchen preparing her lunch. He felt unsure of what steps to take, especially without causing an unnecessary fuss. He surveyed the waiting room where she might be replenishing the gift items. Half the chairs were occupied by dog owners looking at their phones or reading the magazines offered while their dogs of all sizes and levels of patience panted, paced or slept beside them.

Kevin's blood ran cold. There was no sign of Quiznos, but there was of Charity, sitting in a corner seat by the shelf of dog toys and leashes for sale. Her blue cotton blazer livened the drab room with its grey upholstered industrial chairs and beige, pet-proof rug. She was reading *Pet Set*, the tips of her pink fingernails delicately caressing the top of Stella's head as she sat on the floor beside her, tilting back a little, as if to receive the fullest pleasure of her master's touch. As if sensing Kevin's presence, Charity looked up. "Kevin!"

Under the eyes of every person and dog in the waiting room, Charity rose as Kevin approached her. He knew a kiss between them would cause an explosion of barking, and it predictably came. A Rottweiler, a Scottish Terrier and Stella caused such a racket that Rodney came running into the room.

"So what brings you here?" Kevin said to Charity when the previous calm was restored. "I hope Stella's not under the weather."

"No, no. She's fine. She's due for her yearly booster." She looked down at her dog. "Aren't you, honey?"

"You should have told me you were coming. I would have gotten you the royal treatment."

"That's okay. I wanted the full experience of the clinic. You know my workplace, so I should know yours."

For months when speaking with Charity, he had tried his best to avoid the topic of the clinic or his work in it and had perhaps in passing mentioned his employer's name. Nothing good could come of this meeting. But then again, when he took a few seconds to look around him, at the walls, floors and furnishings, he realized his own paranoiac perception. Madness was not something that hung like a sign on the men's room door. It would not stream out of the water cooler tap or color the leaves of the fiddle leaf plant Quiznos kept on her desk. Nowhere within the clinic walls could a total newcomer detect even the slightest hint of insanity. Kevin breathed more freely. There was nothing to worry about. His workplace appeared as ordinary as table salt. When treating his patients, Dr. Ahab conducted himself in only the most professional manner.

Kevin said quietly, "I'll ask Dr. Ahab if he'll see you right away."

"Don't be silly—"

But he was already on his way to the examination room. There he found Rodney holding the Pointer still and Dr. Ahab with a small electric saw in his hands, about to turn it on.

"You got yourself a girl?" the doctor said.

"She's in the waiting room. I was wondering if you could see her—"

"Her dog has fleas?"

"No, I've been checking her periodically. I told you about Stella, the English bulldog on Plymouth Street. She's been clean of fleas for a few weeks now. She's here for a vaccination."

The doctor's eye glimmered with the recollection. "Thorough checks?"

"Yes, thorough."

"No fleas?"

"None."

He flicked the switch on the saw. "She'll have to wait her turn," he called over the noise it made.

XXIV

A REBELLION

Quiznos found herself marching down Brockton Avenue passing the post office, the nail salon and the Nanford Cafe. A fresh breeze rid her lungs of the fetid clinic air. The brilliant, blue sky and puffy, white clouds turned the town into an optimistic setting. She found the moment so dreamlike and pleasurable she felt sure she was doing the right thing and should have done it weeks ago. Then again, she could turn back any time with the excuse she had needed a walk and a candy bar.

When she reached the corner of Brockton and Warwick Streets, she paused before the large plate glass windows of the Nanford Coffee Shop. Its door, emanating the sounds of muzak and clattering tableware, stood invitingly open. Inside, she slid into a two-person booth next to a window overlooking the tables and chairs set up for outdoor dining. She was close enough to the kitchen to enjoy the scent of a savory steam. A waitress in a snug-fitting uniform and poorly applied lipstick greeted her. "Quiznos. You're early for lunch."

"Business is slow." Quiznos took the menu extended to her, though she knew most of it by heart. The air-conditioning began to penetrate her bones, so she asked for a cup of tea and would order the rest when the waitress returned. Minutes later, the hot cup warming her fingers, Quiznos told her, "I'll have the steak, potatoes and dumplings."

"That comes with a cup of soup," the waitress said, as if such a meal would not be enough to satisfy such a petite woman. She pointed to a small card inside the menu that listed the soup options of the day.

"I'll take the chowder," Quiznos said and was pleased when it arrived. It was made of clams and bits of bacon in a hearty tomato base and seasoned with onion and thyme. Oddly enough, her appetite remained unaffected by the protest she was currently conducting—by the loss of a job she had held for twenty-two years—and she found the chowder exceedingly excellent. I must be in denial, she thought, but it's a good denial. And while plying her spoon in the bowl of soup, she wondered if she was becoming a chowderhead.

When the meat arrived, she cut it tenderly, chewed it noiselessly and carefully swallowed it. The French fries had been browned to a perfect crisp. But even as she devoured them, her appetite continued to rage. It seemed hardly possible that by such generous mouthfuls she would not balloon and explode. While chewing her first dumpling, she barely noticed a young man arriving at the table just outside her window accompanied by a sleek Great Dane nearly as large as a small pony, not an ideal dog to bring to an eatery, even to a table outside. Both wore red bandanas around their necks, the extent of their similarities. What the man lacked in size that dog made up for, and his deep black fur made the man's white skin appear even paler. He commanded the dog to lie down, and the dog folded himself up between his table and the next, within Quiznos' sight.

She found the second dumpling so tasty she barely heard the man scolding the dog, but slowly his words entered her consciousness.

"Stop it!" he said. "Junior! Stop scratching."

The dog was lying on his side, his hind paw clawing at his

chest area. Had he been smaller, this activity might have gone barely noticed, but his size caused his every shake to measure what seemed like an eight on the Richter scale. Quiznos was unable to take another bite. The dog was flea infested, and one of these fleas was Moby. But no, she thought. I will not give into that crazy notion. No one can convince me a flea is the cause of this discomfort. Dogs have been scratching themselves since the beginning of time for any number of reasons including dermatitis, an allergy to pollen or mold, a hormonal imbalance or a mild anxiety. And many insects other than fleas aggravate dogs, like ticks and mites. With the third dumpling hanging on her fork, she watched the dog, wishing the scratching would stop, as the young man tried to ignore it, looking over his menu. How am I supposed to enjoy my meal watching this dog in such distress? she thought. Only minutes later, she found herself outside, in conversation with the young man.

When Quiznos returned to the clinic, she found Rodney at her desk talking on the phone. Seeing her, he immediately told her caller to "hold on, please" and extended the receiver to her. "A Mrs. Randolph wants to bring her dog in for a possible euthanasia, she does," he told Quiznos. "I thought you were gone forever. Dr. Ahab was ready to fire you, he was."

"I was scouting out dogs to inspect." Quiznos took the phone, calmed Mrs. Randolph and told her she was doing the right thing. After opening her appointment file, she arranged a date and time for her and her terrier to come in. Then, consulting a paper napkin with a phone number scrawled on it in green ink, she called the young man she had met at the coffee shop and added him and Junior to the schedule.

XXV

A FLEA OF UNCOMMON WHITENESS

Kevin, Rodney and Kit had not walked out on their jobs, but Quiznos' words had woken something deep inside them. The search for Moby, initially preposterous, had over the months become so routine, Kevin now saw it as commonplace as sweeping the floor, and the doctor's monomania, once a terror, as serious as the common cold. Quiznos' words had reminded him that a quest to find a white flea named Moby did not exist anywhere but within the walls of Dr. Ahab's clinic. It would not be spoken about on the six o'clock news nor read about in any newspaper. And if it were, they would have all been carted to a psych ward.

The following Wednesday, Kevin and Rodney were conducting a flea-search on an overweight Pekingese, and Kit, after weeks of trying to convince Dr. Ahab of its importance, sat at the employee room iMac constructing ahabveterinary.com.

"My business has been thriving for years without a webstation," Dr. Ahab had said, becoming suspicious of Kit's extra curricular activities on the computer. But when Rodney told him it would most likely increase his chances of finding Moby, he consented.

"Maybe Quiznos was right about the madness," Kevin said to Rodney as he combed the fat dog's legs, "and we've been in denial. Maybe we've lost sight of it. Maybe we *should* try to put a stop to it."

Rodney's squinty eyes opened wider than Kevin imagined them capable of. "I've been thinking the same thing, I have," he said.

"So we'll abandon Dr. Ahab?"

"No, we don't have to quit. We can save our jobs by being smart, we can. I've been thinking about this all night." Rodney called to Kit, hunched over his keyboard, retouching a photo of the crew to give each a more pleasant look. "Kit, do you have a tube of white paint?"

The following Friday, Kit brought one in.

"Are we really going to do this?" Kevin asked Rodney as Rodney was demonstrating the X-ray machine.

"We have no choice, we don't," Rodney said, while Kevin and Kit lay a sedated dog on the table and arranged it accordingly. "Quiznos was right. This situation is untenable, and we'll be doing the doctor a favor, we will. It doesn't matter the means. We'll be solving the problem and restoring sanity to the office, yes, sanity. The flea is probably long dead by now anyway. We'll be saving the doctor from years of agony, and in the end, if he ever found out what we did, he would thank us, yes, thank us."

They would wait until a dark-haired dog came in, the contrast between its fur and the flea the most preferred for showcasing the insect's whiteness. Finally at three-thirty, a Frank Bulkington, a mountain of a man, arrived with his tiny, black teacup Chihuahua, complaining his dog had a cough and a greenish nasal discharge. Rodney's eyes lit with eagerness at the sight of the dog and imagined a white flea glowing like the moon in her dark fur.

"The flea will be practically the same size as the dog," Kevin said. "Maybe we should wait for a larger one."

"We can't wait forever, we can't," Rodney said. "And this dog is a prefect pitch black."

Frank watched with anxious eyes as Dr. Ahab took the nervous dog's temperature, listened to her heart, examined her ears, eyes and gums then asked about her diet, exercise and elimination patterns, until he was quivering with suspense. The dog had a mild case of canine influenza, the doctor finally said, and needed to be vaccinated. "It's common. Nothing to worry about. I'll prepare the vaccine. If you want to wait outside it'll take a few minutes."

Frank exhaled, "Thank God," and left the examination room. Dr. Ahab quickly administered the shot and, on his way out of the room, said to Kevin and Rodney as he usually did, "Go ahead, men."

Rodney never sounded so eager. "We will," he said, "Yes, we will."

As the dog stood quietly enough, and Rodney picked up the flea comb, Kevin hurried after the doctor. "Dr. Ahab, before you go—" He drew him to the far side of the room.

"I was wondering," Kevin began, "I was wondering. . ." He had not prepared himself thoroughly.

"Yes?" the doctor said, eager to return to his log.

"About the cotton balls. . . "

"The cotton balls? What about them?"

Kevin had no choice but to hope something brilliant would come out of his mouth. He tried to remember what he had once read. "You probably know. . .they're mostly plastic fibers. You can only use them once, and they don't decompose. They get added to the millions of tons of plastics thrown into the ocean every year. They're destroying marine life, giving brain damage to fish. Maybe we should find some other. . .some substitute. . . for . . ?"

For a few seconds Dr. Ahab gave Kevin a dumb stare. "Cotton balls are destroying marine life? Are we more concerned with the fish than the dogs? What do you suggest I use? The back of my hand?"

Kevin had no answer, but as he once again opened his mouth praying for words, not a second too late, Rodney called out, "The White Flea! It's him! I've found him!"

"Stay calm, stay calm," Dr. Ahab said. In no time he was peering at the dog's rear back as Rodney separated the tufts of hair there to display his 'discovery.' There the flea lay, lifeless and gleaming in the overhead lights.

Dr. Ahab peered so closely at it, he might have breathed it back alive. "Don't move a muscle," he said. "Keep the dog still. Don't lose sight of it. Bring me a comb. And a paper towel."

"Is it Moby?" Kit said, hurrying over.

"I think it is!" Rodney handed the doctor his comb. "I remember him, I do! A large flea with long legs and a round back. I could never forget that flea, never! Can you, Dr. Ahab? It's him, isn't it? It's him. Someone tell Quiznos! We've found Moby, we have!"

But the doctor needed a closer look. "Shhhhh! We'll see."

The little dog, frightened by all the attention, began to squirm. Rodney held her while Dr. Ahab put down the comb and picked the flea out of her dark fur with the tips of his right thumb and index finger. He opened his thumb to examine it closely then spun away from the light. He transferred it to the top of his left index finger and turned around again.

"The White Flea, yes, Dr. Ahab?" Rodney wished he wouldn't handle it quite so much.

"It's Moby, right?" Kevin said as Dr. Ahab once again transferred the flea from finger to finger.

"I'll tell Quiznos," Kit slowly backed out of the examination room.

But the paint had not been the quick drying kind. By this time it had rubbed completely off, and the bug once again appeared brown. When Kit and Quiznos entered in the room, they found the doctor agitated.

"It's not him," he said, standing at the sink, rinsing the flea off his finger. "Again, it was just the light. Please stop wasting my time." He headed once more to his office.

XXVI

A CONFESSION

Kevin's meetings with Charity at the dog park had become so routine he had long stopped giving them a second thought. He was simply required to be there at 7 p.m. on Tuesdays and Fridays and had always prided himself on his ability to fulfill social obligations, not to mention his promptness. But the following Monday, he received an ominous email from Charity requesting his presence there at lunchtime without his dog. The change in their routine, the urgency of her message and the omission of Weewag could only mean one thing. He tried to replay in his mind his last encounter with her and could think of no offense he had committed.

He was prepared for the worst but clueless as to the cause. Her conversation and eagerness to see him had always implied a deep fondness for him. She had generally taken great interest in what troubles and concerns he had chosen to reveal to her. Had she only been play-acting? He hadn't seen her since her visit to the clinic. Maybe she had been repelled by Rodney's Spock ears. Or had she been able to sniff out Dr. Ahab's lunacy?

Kevin hastened from the clinic to the dog park hoping whatever Charity wanted to discuss would not take the entire hour and would leave him time to return home and walk with Weewag. It was an unusually cool day for the end of August. Black clouds hung ominously low in the windless sky. The park stood barren and desolate, clean of stained tennis balls and the smell of urine. Only three dog owners sat a good distance from each other studying their phones while their dogs roamed independently. Kevin sighted Charity sitting on their usual bench glancing downward, her posture poor, her hair, usually shiny and bouncy, in stringy strands. Though not a drop of rain had yet fallen, her light grey raincoat was tightly belted with its collar up. Without Stella she looked incomplete, as if she were missing an arm or a leg.

When he sat next to her, he was surprised to feel his hackles rise. And why not? No serious talk—as this one was sure to be —ever ended well. But no, he told himself, this time will be different. I am not so invested. Even if I were head over heels for Charity, I would react to whatever words she uttered with complete composure. A thick callous now protected his heart. A quart of ice cream lay ready in his freezer. His long list of comedies was waiting to be streamed.

She took his hand, the first sign his prediction might prove correct. Her voice fluttered. "It's good to see you."

"It's good to see you too. What's the matter? What did you have to tell me?"

"It's not easy," she said. "I wrote it down then rehearsed it, then I tore it up. I don't want to say the wrong thing."

"It's better to say *something*," Kevin said. "Go ahead."

She gathered her wits and eyed him head on. "As much as I adore you, as much as spending time with you has always been a little piece of heaven, I've made up my mind. I can't see you anymore. I'm tired of being dishonest. I can't continue these deceptions." She took a breath. "In my heart of hearts I can never love you as much as I love Stella." Even through the thick lenses of her glasses, he could see her eyes grow pink and watery as she continued, her voice unsteady. "Stella is everything to me. She's my guide through life's torments, the light in my darkness, my therapist and my priest. She wakens my soul and helps me breathe. When she barks I hear the notes of a symphony." She finished her sentence just before a sob overtook her, and when her composure returned, she went on. "I don't know how I came to this point. I never thought when I became a dog owner this would happen. You're not the first person I've had to tell this to, and now I can't see an end to it." The tip of her nose pinkened, and she sniffed loudly. She removed her glasses to wipe her tears as they ran down her cheeks.

Kevin, having hung on to her every word, grit his teeth, waiting for his forehead to burst with sweat or his stomach to somersault. But so far his blood flowed calmly, his heart beat with its usual rhythm and he felt his lungs normally inflating and deflating.

Charity honked into a Kleenex then dabbed at the bottom of her nose. "I'm sorry, Kevin. I would give anything to be able to change how I feel. But what can I do? Are you all right?" She gave him an expectant look.

"I don't know," he said slowly, wondering if it were possible to receive these words without some reaction.

"Tell me. I can help you. I don't want you to feel bad."

He waited a few seconds. "But I don't feel bad. I mean, yes, I'm sorry to hear it. I would have liked things to be otherwise, but I think I'll be okay. As a matter of fact, I completely understand. I feel exactly the same about Weewag. I had a hunch about it for a while, but I was waiting to see if it was true."

There, he had said the thing that had been sitting in the back of his mind from the very start. He held his breath, prepared for perhaps more tears. But her cheeks rounded and her eyes narrowed with a smile. "You do?" Her voice rose with what sounded like joy. "God, I'm so relieved. For a minute there I thought I was the only freak, the only oddball—"

"Maybe there are more of us around than we think," Kevin said.

Ever since Kevin met Charity, he felt Weewag tugging at one arm and Charity at the other until he feared he might split in half. But it was Weewag who triumphed. It was Weewag who made no demands on Kevin, who gave Kevin his full attention, who didn't criticize his lifestyle, his choice of employment or his plans for the future. Weewag had no concern for the future. He would support Kevin in whatever path he chose and would walk beside him down that path for as long as their legs could carry them. And if they were lucky, they would reach the end of that path together.

She threw her arms around him. "I love you for not choosing me over your dog," she said. "I love you for not loving me!"

"Let's not get carried away."

Charity kissed Kevin's cheek. "Goodbye, Kevin. I hope you and Weewag are happy together."

"And I hope you and Stella are too."

"But we can see each other in the dog park, can't we?"

"We will."

She paused a few seconds then looked at him dreamily. "If only you were a dog, Kevin, then everything would be perfect!"

XXVII

KEVIN AND WEEWAG

Though Kevin did not feel the loss of specifically Charity, he began to feel the loss of someone, especially someone capable of giving him more than what Weewag could. As the days passed, days of flea searching and trying to please his troubled employer, and even as he spent enjoyable evenings with his beloved pet, Kevin began to experience feelings of stagnation and immobility, that nothing gleamed over the horizon. Charity had woken up a craving for his own kind. Weewag could supply him with a lifetime of adoration, loyalty and affection, but Kevin could only enjoy interspecies love to a point. This once minor frustration was growing in his mind. His dog would never be able to tell him what shirt he looked best in or which presidential candidate he preferred. The highs and lows that once came with close human companionship were growing in appeal. He craved some kind of argument, no matter how petty or acrimonious. His determination to fight the dictates of society were weakening, and he was recognizing that for the sake of his own happiness he had no choice but to conform to at least some of them. His doubts about his relationship with Weewag were now confirmed, that the dog was turning Kevin asocial and hermetic. Weewag was preventing him from living a normal life.

Kevin could not have anticipated such a tight bond forming between them, and perhaps this realization had come too late.

Maybe he had already lost the ability to bond with another human being, and he had become more keenly in tune with the physical rather than the metaphysical world. It was possible he had developed a keener sensitivity to body language than speech intonations and, as he walked down the street, had become more aware of the intensity of the sun, the humidity in the air and the smell of the scant grass or flowers that managed to grow in Nanford's rocky soil.

When one day at home, out of the corner of his eye, Kevin saw his dog scampering towards him with his tug toy in his mouth, he pretended to be involved in his book. Another day, sitting alone on a bench in the dog park, he watched him glee-fully galloping towards him, as if unable to withstand even ten minutes away from him. It was then that Kevin knew Weewag had to be sacrificed.

Back home, he scoured the contract he had signed when he had adopted the dog. "If for any reason the adopter is unable to keep this dog," he read, "he will immediately notify the pound, and we will work with him to find the appropriate home for this dog. Transfer of ownership of this dog is strictly prohibit-ed without prior written authorization of the pound."

The following Saturday morning, Kevin packed Weewag's bed, toys and a few remaining cans of dog food into a travel-ing bag, attached his leash to his collar then followed him as he scrambled down the stairs and out onto the sidewalk, as if to take yet another pleasant walk perhaps to the dog park. It was a fine, sunny day. The early September air, though still warm, had lost its humidity and was filled with an earthy aro-ma. Though few leaves would be shed from Nanford's small number of trees, Kevin knew fall was arriving. The seasons were changing, and with that change came new hopes and resolutions.

As he guided his dog north on Manhattan Street, he greeted his mailman then the woman with the Irish Setter they sometimes ran into who stopped to chat about a new organic dog food she had found. Her dog was feisty, impatiently pulling on his leash while Weewag sat quietly. "You're lucky to have found such a wonderful dog," she said before they parted.

As they continued on their way, Weewag glanced back at Kevin as he sometimes did, but his mouth seemed set in a grimace, his eyes appeared wide with fear, and he suddenly fell to pulling on his leash in the opposite direction. But soon Kevin realized he was only expressing an urgency to sniff a particular fire hydrant, which he allowed for longer than usual. Moving on, as he watched Weewag's furry tail sway as he walked ahead of him, and as his sleek dark coat gleamed in the sun, Kevin told himself, this is all for the best. And he reviewed in his mind all the justifications for his action, increasing his confidence in his decision. And if I'm asked why I'm returning him, he thought, I'll make it plain he's pleasant and well-behaved and would make an excellent pet for any other owner, but that my busy life makes it impossible to give him the care and attention he needs. I have to be absolutely sure euthanasia is not in his future. If so, I'll take him back immediately.

Weewag turned again and gave him a look filled with so much love and trust, Kevin almost collapsed with shame. What on earth am I doing? he thought. Does this have anything to do with the insanity in Dr. Ahab's clinic? It's seeped into my mind and destroyed my ability to think with any kind of logic or clarity. Kevin could hardly believe he had become so unhinged that he would give up the one being in his life that grounded him, that kept him stable, his main source of pleasure and well-being. It was the quest for Moby that was driving him, that had made him unable to fall for Charity, that compelled him to give up his pet. But no, he had no right to blame Dr. Ahab for his problems. He himself was their sole instigator.

They passed other dog walkers who patiently waited while their dogs relieved themselves then picked up their droppings the same way they might pick up a fallen rose, people who had managed to attain healthy relationships with their pets, relationships that involved mutual respect for boundaries and allowed both members the freedom to relate to other humans or dogs, something Kevin had miserably failed to do. He should not have placed Weewag in the center of his life, and now it was too late. He was unable to unlove his pet. He was only able to give him away.

The closer they came to the decrepit building, the more Kevin's pace slowed and, when still at some distance from it, he came to a full stop. No, I must go on, he told himself. I made this decision with a completely clear head for the most sensible, pragmatic reason. He quickened his pace to make sure he would not change his mind before reaching the door. But after climbing the few steps that lead to it, when he tried to swing it open, it wouldn't budge. The pound was closed. At first a wave of relief passed over him, then a feeling of dismay. He would have to repeat the ordeal all over again.

"Labor Day weekend," a passerby told Kevin as he stood with one hand still clutching the door handle, paralyzed on the top step. He watched his dog sniffing the steps until Weewag's eyes met his, and he wagged his tail as if to say, "Let's go home." The poor, innocent creature should not be anywhere near this building, Kevin thought. How could I have even considered taking him back inside it? No, he would not be able to repeat this effort. He had blamed Weewag for his own shortcomings. There was no reason he couldn't love both Weewag and another human being at the same time. The problem was Kevin, not Weewag.

Here was proof of his total isolation and alienation from everyday life. Because dog illnesses can occur at any time, Dr. Ahab insisted the clinic be open every day of the week including weekends and holidays. So removed from the real world, only the day before, not one of his co-workers had even mentioned Labor Day. Trotting after Weewag as they made their way home, though he tried, he was unable to picture Dr. Ahab, Quiznos, Rodney or even Kit at a barbecue.

XXVIII

SELF-DOUBT

Most of all, Dr. Ahab. He was at the same time existing in the world and taking no part in it. Holidays, sports events, films and other entertainments had now joined the detritus of society littering some faraway planet he no longer stood on. He could most often be found sitting before his iMac, scouring and scanning the list of local dogs he had not yet examined, trying to conquer its infiniteness, to rid his soul of the poison that plagued him and restore his faith in the world.

One day when his office door was open, Quiznos saw the bent old man and heard in her heart the sobbing around him. Careful not to draw his attention, she stood in his doorway.

Dr. Ahab turned and looked up. "Quiznos!"

"Doctor." She took a step inside.

"Quiznos, on a day very much like today, a boy of eighteen, I killed my first flea. Fifty years ago! From then on, forsaking all else, I devoted myself to the care and well-being of animals. When I think of the life I have led, the heaviness, the weariness, the solitude! When I think of how for years, I ate my lonely sandwich at my desk, fit emblem of the dry nourishment of my soul! I subsist on moldy crusts when other doctors dine out in the finest restaurants. When I think of the son I have lost and the poor woman I married one day then abandoned the next without a honeymoon and with only a dent in her pillow. I widowed the poor girl, then murdered her with my neglect. And then I think of the madness, the frenzy, the boiling blood and the smoking brow with which I have furiously chased a prey—more a demon. What a fool I have been! Why burden myself with such a chase? Why wear out my fingers with the spray bottle? How much richer or better would it make me? Quiznos, is it not surprising that with this weary load I bear, one poor eye should be snatched away from me? Brush this old hair aside. It blinds me. Stand close to me and let me look into a human eye instead of those of a dog. I know what you think of my quest. I pray you don't leave me, but you're not obliged to stay. The risk is not yours to take."

She was staid, steadfast and devoted to Dr. Ahab. She had for some time resumed her natural disposition, but her opposition to his quest remained strong. "Doctor, you stubborn man! Why should anyone chase after that horrible insect? Let it go already! Let it go right now! You have to get rid of this negativity!"

But Dr. Ahab averted his glance. Like a sick plant shaking off its last dead leaf, he shook his head. "Why do I keep pushing myself to do what in my heart I know is wrong? The flea must have died months ago, yet my mania persists. I can't stop wearing myself out searching for a thing so tiny it couldn't possibly hold a tenth of the malice I impose on it. It's madness that drives me, that makes me a stranger to myself. Whose arm lifts the spray bottle? Whose voice commands these endless flea searches? The AVMA should bar me from my clinic doors. I'm placing a risk on the livelihood and the sanity of my workers. I'm driven by a force stronger than myself I'm unable to conquer."

But pale and shaken, Quiznos had long left the room.

XXIX

WEEWAG FALLS ILL

A few days later, Weewag was overtaken by a strange lethargy. He caught a terrible chill that lapsed into a fever. Poor Weewag! An indomitable woe stole over Kevin as he sat by his waning pet. Mysterious shades crept over the dog. For a few days, he lay on his blanket wasting away until there seemed nothing left of him but his frame. His food lay untouched in his bowl. His cheekbones grew sharp. His eyes, plagued by unusual yellow incrustations, took on an odd luster and, like circles on the water which, as they grow fainter, expand, they seemed to grow rounder, like rings of eternity. Weewag was close to death's door.

Kevin attached his leash to his collar, but the poor dog was barely able to walk. He had no choice but to carry him to Dr. Ahab's clinic. The doctor's years of experience and expertise would surely lead to a diagnosis and cure.

The deep affection between Kevin and his pet had caused him to forget the doctor's mania. He should have made an appointment with any other veterinarian. No sooner did they step into the examination room than the doctor's one eye lit like a searchlight at the sight of another potential host of his tiny demon pest. Kevin prayed he would not be distracted from finding the actual cause of Weewag's distress, that he would carry out the cure and not a single trace of any flea would be discovered in his fur.

As they set Weewag on the examination table, Quiznos joined them, and Kit kept an eye on them. More than six months had passed since Kevin and Weewag had first visited the clinic, but the doctor showed no recollection of the dog. To Kevin's relief, he began his examination in his usual manner, using his stethoscope, otoscope and thermometer. But then the worst came to pass. Dr. Ahab thrust out his face fiercely sniffing.

"What do you smell?" Kevin asked, barely able to conceal the dread in his voice. Soon the peculiar odor emitted by fleas, sometimes even to a great distance, was palpable. Dr. Ahab ran his fingers through the dog's hairs, thoroughly checking his neck, back and legs, then turned Weewag over. After a minute he froze, as if embedded in ice.

He spoke in a hushed voice. "Get me the Perthacide."

"The Perthacide? But what about his lack of appetite, his lethargy? Certainly, fleas have nothing to do with that."

"Bring me the Perthacide. And you take the Doom. Quiznos, the Demon Killer."

Kevin and Quiznos quickly did as the doctor requested then joined him looking down at the ailing dog.

"What do you see?" Dr. Ahab asked.

"Nothing, sir," Kevin said.

The doctor spread the hairs on the left side. "I saw something white. A flash, a rush. Do you see it?"

"See what?" Quiznos said, looking closely. The pink skin of the dog's belly lay as smooth as still waters.

"There he is! A hump like a snow hill. Could it be—"

Months of fruitless combing for the hated flea had soured Kevin's hopes. Twice he had mistaken a brown flea for a white one. He gave a better look. Something tiny and white was indeed there, half hidden in the brown hairs on the left side of the dog's stomach. Could it be that concealed within the tufts of his own pet he was beholding the infamous insect they had so long pursued? His mind strained to replay the countless encounters on their walks and in the dog park between Weewag and other neighborhood dogs. They had sniffed and wagged their tails at each other, many times making contact. It was highly possible one of these encounters involved the transfer of fleas.

He and Quiznos peered closely at the dog's underside. Dr. Ahab spread the hairs wide to reveal a scurrying insect. Could it be true? Like a tiny pearl it traveled the jagged landscape of fur. Kevin's forehead felt hot. Quiznos held onto the back of a chair.

Dr. Ahab spoke in a hoarse whisper. "It is he! The White Flea!" He held his bottle aimed and ready. "There he goes! I'd recognize him anywhere. He's heading over the stomach. Stand by, Kevin." He turned to Kit. "Kit, give us back up."

"Kit?" Kevin said. "Where's Rodney?"

"Yes, Kit," the doctor said. "Kit, get the Nuke 'Em"

With much reluctance, Kit rose and soon joined them holding the can assigned to him, his head slightly turned away. But his curiosity soon won the better of him. He took a quick look and his cheeks flushed. "It's the White Flea!"

Yes, it was Moby, running to where the hairs began to thicken, revealing his high, sparkling hump. "He's heading to the leg," Kevin said. A gentle joyousness, a mighty repose in swiftness propelled the rushing bug.

"Quiet," Dr. Ahab said. "Get ready." A death glimmer lit his sunken eyes. A hideous motion gnawed his mouth. The fur lay as smooth and serene as dark waters. At length the flea's dazzling hump could be seen rushing through the brown fleece along the upper right leg, accompanied by a chaotic ripple.

Dr. Ahab, allured by this scuttle, ventured to assail him, but the hump submerged, and he lowered his bottle. "Hurry on, Flea. We're not afraid to follow you."

The dog's hairs waved on as the flea still withheld from sight, entirely hiding his wretched hideousness. But soon he reemerged, and for an instant, his whole marbleized body formed a high arch, then just as quickly, he again disappeared.

All readied their weapons maintaining the profoundest silence, waiting for the next appearance.

Then Quiznos said, "I see him running down the leg!"

"Where?" Kit said, sneaking another look.

"Yes, there he is," Dr. Ahab said. "He's creating an infallible wake. Follow that wake. Steady! Were it a brand-new world, there couldn't be a fairer day. Here is food for thought —if I had time to think, but I never think. I only feel and that's enough. Kevin, what do you see?"

"Nothing, sir."

"Nothing! So it is. I've over chased him. He's chasing me now. I might have guessed it."

Suspenseful moments flew by, the insect resurfaced, and all shrieked as if their tongues were on fire.

"He's turned around and is heading towards the armpit," Quiznos murmured. "I feel sick to my stomach."

"I see him, I see him," Kit said, raising his can high, his finger ready on the valve.

"Stand by to back me up!" Dr. Ahab cried. "He's emerged once more!"

The White Flea darted through the weltering sea of hair up

the dog's right side with the utmost velocity, as if bent on escaping his host's body.

"Dr. Ahab," Quiznos cried, "it's not too late, even now, to call off your chase. See! The flea doesn't care about you. You're the one pursuing him like a madman!"

The determined doctor was suddenly distracted by the entrance of Rodney arriving to pick up his paycheck. He hailed him to grab the can of Demon Killer, and soon Rodney joined them looking down at Kevin's pet.

"Moby!" he gasped and stood ready with the rest, eyes intent on the flea as he swiftly shot to the surface again. He veered this way and that across the dog's stomach towards his ribcage, barely visible, his crustaceous body strangely vibrating, propelled by retribution, vengeance and malice.

"I shoot first," Dr. Ahab cried. "Forehead to forehead I meet you again, Moby the Flea! Kevin! Quiznos! Brace up! Crowd him!" With back arched and arm lifted high, Dr. Ahab pulled hard on his trigger, sending his fierce spray and curse onto the hated insect, soon barely seen in a smoky mist that curled around the doctor's magisterial nose.

"The head!" Quiznos' voice emerged from within the cloud. "Doctor, the head's emerging!"

"Again, attack!" Dr. Ahab's voice rose as he sprayed on. "You who strikes a defenseless dog won't land me in a coffin or hearse. Only vengeance could kill me! Ha!"

When the vapor cleared, the flea, maddened and weighted by the burst of insecticides and seemingly possessed, churned over the ribs, shedding specks of spray from his narrow back until he once more immersed himself into the dog's thick hairs.

"He's moved into the safety of the armpit, a better if a bitterer hiding place." Dr. Ahab took a few seconds to look up and around him. "Goodbye, old clinic! The walls are peeling. Green mold falls on my head! Quiznos, we grow old together, me, minus an eye. The business of tending to animals is sound, though we are not. I know vets older than me that will live longer. Keep a good eye on the flea when I'm gone. Let me know when you see him lying there, asphyxiated, head to pygidium." He hovered over the dog. "Quiznos!"

"Doctor!"

"Some men die confronting the smallest adversary, some with spray cans, some with their own concoction. My bottle is emptying. I am old. Shake hands with me, Quiznos."

Their hands met. Their eyes fastened, Quiznos' tears the glue. "Doctor, leave him alone already! Even brave men some-times weep!"

"Stand by!" Dr. Ahab cried, tossing her hand from his. "Stand by, Kevin, Rodney!"

"Heart of steel!" Quiznos murmured, gazing at Dr. Ahab. "Don't you realize what you're doing, chasing a flea like this? I feel calm and tormented at the same time! I can't see past or future. Kevin! See the doctor's hand on the trigger?
He's not in his right mind! Keep your eye on his enemy. Pay attention to it! Help him drive off that bug!"

"Ready, Quiznos, Kevin, Kit? Are you with us Rodney?" Dr. Ahab cried. "These old hands are useless now and will never improve. When he plans to attack, I'm ready to die. You are my arms and legs, so obey me. Where's the flea? Gone again?"

As cans and bottle lowered, Quiznos cried, "The flea, the flea! There he is!" Crawling over and under tufts of fur, Moby scurried down the dog's left side.

"Sit tight! Who can tell," Dr. Ahab said, "whether he aims to feast on the dog or me?"

The White Flea ventured once more onto the dog's stomach where the hairs grew the thinnest. Whether tired by the chase or by some latent deceitfulness and malice inside him, his pace began to slow.

"Get ready!" Quiznos said. "He's turning as if he wants to meet us! Doctor? He knows he can't win."

Dr. Ahab looked from face to face. "Don't stand by me, but under me, you who help me," he said. "Kit, too, sticks with me." He looked down again at his adversary as the bug continued his manic course. "I grin at you, you grinning flea! For all you have done, I would still clink glasses with you, if you wanted! Oh, flea, there'll be plenty of dying soon! Why don't you accept it, Moby, accept the death coming to you, a most toxic and chemical death. The voyage is up!"

Suddenly the dog's stomach upheaved, as if a volcano were erupting inside it. The flea, as if aware his foe was near, presented his entire body with all its whiteness. Crouching on his hind legs, head high, he maliciously waited. It was either his own death or the death of his enemy. His blind defense knew no other options, no excuses, no thought.

"Rodney!" the doctor cried. "Let me hear your heart beating. Am I cut off from the pride of the most beaten-down vets? Oh, lonely death, lonely life! My greatness lies in my grief. From near and far, pour in, you black cloud of life, and help me overcome this threat! I'm ready to battle you, you menacing flea. To the last I grapple with you. From hell's heart I spray you. For hate's sake I spit my last breath at you. No coffin or hearse waits for me, you damned flea! I shoot!"

A low rumble rose from the doctor's throat, a subterraneous hum as all held their breaths. He pulled hard on his trigger, and all were shrouded in a drooping veil of mist.

Through it, Kevin could barely make out a shadow in the form of his dog. Surely, he thought, his ailing lungs could not withstand the toxic spray. But as if out of a deep sleep, the shadow lurched forward and shook with all its might. Through the dimness, Kevin saw the red leash shoot high into the air with igniting velocity. The hazy figure of Dr. Ahab stooped to clear it, but to no avail. The flying leather looped twice around the doctor's neck, and the dog, in a great effort to leap off the table, pulled hard in the opposite direction, constricting the passage of the old man's breath. Still trying to escape the poisonous fog, Weewag maintained that pull. All hands reached to help Dr. Ahab, but the vapor's thickness prevented clear sight.

Out of the mist came a raspy cry. "I grow blind! Quiznos, guide me! Or I must grope my own way. Is it night?" As the air grew clearer, all could better discern the doctor, his hands gripping the noose that bound his throat.

"Weewag!" Kevin cried.

Rodney cried, "Doctor!"

Kevin rushed to unhook the leash from his dog's collar and took him in his arms. He turned to join the others, trying to unbind the deadly restraint from the doctor's neck. But it was too late. Dr. Ahab sank to the floor.

Quiznos swooped down to attend to him as the rest gathered around. She put her ear to his chest.

"Is his heart beating?" Rodney said in a whisper.

"Is he all right?" Kevin said.

"What do you hear?" Kit asked.

"Shhhh!" Soon she lifted her head and slowly rose. "He's gone," she declared.

For an instant they stood tranced, fixed by admiration, fidelity or fate. Rodney took out his phone and dialed 911.

XXX

RESOLUTION

After the medics covered Dr. Ahab's lifeless body with a sheet and wheeled him out on a stretcher, the crew solemnly bid each other goodbye and one by one left the clinic, pale and silent. Kevin remained in the examination room and took the opportunity to inspect his dog for any remaining fleas. He found none and no trace of the White Flea anywhere. Paralyzed by the doctor's spray, Moby had most likely fallen to the ground only to join the detritus of lint and dog hair there. Kevin knelt to survey the floor around and beneath the table, then stepped heavily on all spots where the insect could have landed.

He tucked Weewag once again into his knapsack and headed back home. Considering the possibility that the flea had been flattened on the bottom of his shoe, he stopped at a curb to scrape his sole against it and pictured the tiny crushed body sitting there until the next rain shower washed it into the street. There, a parking car might run over it, its treads a fitting graveyard.

Kevin couldn't fathom why, of all dogs in Nanford, Moby had been found on Weewag. Considering the dog's kindness and consideration—which might have extended to the end of each hair of his coat—he understood why any parasitic insect would choose him. He must have offered a cozier and more comfortable home than other dogs, or the flea more enjoyed the rhythm of his heartbeat or the pulsing of his blood, which may have been tastier. But he couldn't help wondering if it were mere coincidence that off all the dogs in Nanford, it was his own dog who had delivered Moby to the doctor. And if not, he could only deduce something in the realm of the supernatural, that Kevin and Weewag had been chosen by some benevolent power to bring Moby to his employer in order to relieve the old man's pain. If it were not for the woman in the pound recommending Dr. Ahab to Kevin, Dr. Ahab might have been searching for Moby for perpetuity, and she had been chosen as well. But Kevin would not allow himself to follow this path of contemplation lest he continue back to his break-up with Amanda or his parents never having met or the universe never having been created. The unbearable situation in the clinic had come to an end, and he was glad for his part in it.

Weewag seemed to require no further medical attention. The luster returned to his eyes, he was regaining his strength, and after a few days he began eating with a vigorous appetite. One day he suddenly leapt to his feet, gave himself a good stretch and barked as if to say, "I'm better."

Quiznos informed Dr. Ahab's patients of the end of his veterinary practice and referred them to Dr. Goney who appreciated the increase in clientele. She swore she would never work for a veterinarian again and planned to move in with her sister in Fordbed, ten miles away, and help take care of her three young children. Kevin would look for new employment soon, but for the time being was content to spend his days with Weewag.

Kevin knew that whatever is truly wondrous in a dog has never been put into books or words. Besides showing his superiority at catching a ball or playing hide-and-seek, Weewag provided as much entertainment as any form of drama or comedy. He was a king among dogs with a wild whimsiness and a sympathetic soul. He was a riddle to unfold, a wondrous work in one volume, a volume of unsolvable mysteries.

Some days they met Charity and Stella at the dog park where Kevin and Charity sat on a bench watching their pets interact with the lively groups of dogs who gathered there regularly, running, playing, sniffing, urinating and scratching.

Made in the USA
Middletown, DE
11 July 2021

43702350R00097